T038093

BLACKLION

BLACKLION

LUKE FRANCIS BEIRNE

Baraka
Books

Montréal

ISBN 978-1-77186-331-5 pbk; 978-1-77186-333-9 epub; 978-1-77186-334-6 pdf

Cover by Maison 1608
Book Design by Folio infographie
Editing and proofreading: Blossom Thom, Robin Philpot, Anne Marie Marko

Legal Deposit, 3rd quarter 2023
Bibliothèque et Archives nationales du Québec
Library and Archives Canada

Published by Baraka Books of Montreal

Printed and bound in Quebec

Trade Distribution & Returns
Canada – UTP Distribution: UTPdistribution.com

United States
Independent Publishers Group: IPGbook.com

We acknowledge the support from the Société de développement des entreprises culturelles (SODEC) and the Government of Quebec tax credit for book publishing administered by SODEC.

Charlotte, will you marry me?

Is acher in gaíth in-nocht,
fu·fúasna fairggae findfholt;
ní·ágor réimm Mora Minn
dond láechraid lainn úa Lothlind.

(Bitter is the wind tonight,
it stirs up the white-waved sea.
I do not fear the coursing of the Irish sea
by the fierce warriors of Lothlind.)

- Anonymous (c. 800s)

PROLOGUE

RAGGED OLD FLAG

The sheer curtains on the window above the sink blew gently and the black and grey Indiana radio sitting on the corner of the kitchen counter played quietly.

I walked through a county courthouse square
On a park bench an old man was sitting there

Garlic was in the air with the smooth Cash drawl, dense but soft. In the living room off the kitchen, the television played silently. The knife in his hand was light and sharp. He wiped the remaining droplets from the curved blade with the drying cloth and slipped it back into the wooden block beside the radio.

The onions, mushrooms, and garlic began to soften and he shifted them with the spatula, then dropped the steak into the pan beside them. The oil in the pan licked at the edges of the meat, pink turned brown. He put the spatula down, lifted the lid on the potatoes and checked the largest with the prongs of a fork.

The doorbell rang. He set the lid back on the pot and turned to look, though the door was out of view from where he stood. He wiped his hands on the cloth and tossed it onto the countertop beside the radio.

And the south wind blew hard on
That Ragged Old Flag

He went to the front door through the living room. Gerald Ford was on the screen—talking about Nixon, no doubt. Mopping up the messes of the previous administration. He looked through the window. A black Oldsmobile cruiser sat at the curb. He ran his hands through his hair and glanced down at his clothes: blue flannel, white t-shirt, and jeans.

When he got to the door, he could see Nelson's silhouette through the fogged glass panels. He turned the handle and opened it. "Nelson," he said. "How are you?"

"Ray."

"Come in," Ray said. "Don't rush but I've got a steak in the pan."

"Go on," Nelson said. "Don't overcook it on my account."

Ray went back into the kitchen and turned the steak in the pan. "Have you eaten?" he asked. "I have another steak in the fridge."

"I'm alright," Nelson said, coming into the kitchen. He stood there with his hands in the pockets of his black pants, his black coat fell around them like a cape.

"I'll have to eat this before it gets cold," Ray said. He moved the onions and mushrooms and garlic onto the top of the steak and let them soak.

"That's alright. Go ahead."

"You sure you won't eat something?" Ray asked, turning away from the pan. "I have potatoes." He glanced at the stovetop. "No vegetables but I've got more onions and mushrooms."

"You have a beer?" Nelson asked.

"Yeah, in the fridge."

Nelson took his hands out of his pockets and opened the fridge. He stooped down and looked inside. "You want one?" he asked.

"Yeah, give me one of them."

Nelson took out two cans of Old Milwaukee and set one down on the counter beside Ray. Ray passed him the opener and Nelson punched the top of the can. He punched his own and then took the pan off the burner and turned off the heat. He drained the potatoes and got a plate from the cabinet above the radio.

"Take your coat off, Nelson," Ray said. "You're making me nervous."

"Sorry," Nelson said. He slipped his coat off and threw it over an empty section of the countertop.

They sat down at the table in the dining room and Ray began to eat. "How's Anne?"

"She's alright."

"That's alright, then."

Ray ate slowly and carefully and Nelson sat across from him, watching with the beer in his hand. "I guess you're wondering why I'm here," Nelson said eventually.

"I was wondering when you'd get to telling me, anyway."

"It's not about that," Nelson said, gesturing to the television in the corner.

"That's good," Ray said. He set his knife down and picked up the can of beer.

"You're Irish, aren't you, Ray?"

Ray nodded, though he knew that Nelson already knew the answer to that—already knew everything about him.

"You ever been over?"

Ray shook his head, suddenly aware where this was going.

"Have you ever thought about going over?"

"Can't really say that I have, Nelson."

Nelson took another drink then rolled the curve of the can on the tabletop. "We'd like you to go to Ireland, Ray."

Ray cut another piece off the steak and put it in his mouth. Soft, tender, a hint of mineral.

"I know you just got home, so I wouldn't be asking if I had a choice. We need a man over there."

Ray knew that he wasn't asking at all. He thought about Laos. About the river and the heat and the stink of the earth after the rain. "In the embassy?"

"No," Nelson said. "We want it clean. No contact with the embassy. On the ground."

"Clandestine?"

Nelson nodded.

"When?"

"Six weeks."

"How long?"

"It's hard to say, Ray. You know that."

"Will I be illegal?"

"That'll all be in the briefing."

"Will I be illegal, Nelson?"

"Yeah, Ray. You'll be illegal."

Ray nodded.

"There's too much potential for blowback," Nelson said. He finished the beer and set the hollow can down. "But, don't worry. We're not going to leave you naked."

"When do you want me in?"

"Can you come in on Monday?"

"What day is it? Friday?"

"Friday, yeah."

"Yeah," Ray said. "I'll come in on Monday."

"Alright, Ray," Nelson said. He stood up and went into the kitchen. He set the empty can beside the sink and came back into the room with his coat. "I know you must've been looking forward to some rest. Thanks for taking this so well."

"Whatever you say, boss."

Nelson slipped his arms into the sleeves and draped the coat back over his shoulders. He went through the dining room to the front hall. He clapped Ray on the shoulder as he passed. Then he opened the door and stepped out and shut it behind him.

Ray put down his knife and fork and stared at the half-eaten steak on the plate in front of him and thought about Laos.

Slow swinging chopper blades and beams of yellow light falling through shuddering wet leaves; the search for an army of ghosts by men who didn't exist.

He picked up the beer and finished it and went back to the fridge for another. He went back to the table and finished the steak. The potatoes and onions were cold. He brought the plate back into the kitchen and set it beside the sink.

He stood in the kitchen for a while, staring at nothing. Then he went to the yellow phone on the wall, holding the beer in his left hand, and lifted it from the hook. He dialed and waited, listening to the tinny distant sound. There was no answer on the other end.

He hung up the phone and stood there leaning against the wall sipping the beer until the can was empty. Then he set it down beside the other empties next to the sink and grabbed his keys from the table and his coat from the hook beside the door.

It was growing dark already as he crossed from the door to the driveway. He put the key in the door and unlocked the car—a '73 Buick Riviera Stage 1 in Riviera Plum, brand new when he bought it.

He got in and put the key in the ignition and turned it—listened to the engine rumble to life, felt the vibration beneath him coursing through his legs. Willie Nelson started playing from the stereo as the sharp smell of gasoline rose through the body of the car.

And Heaven ain't walking
On a street paved with gold
And Hell ain't no mountain of fire

He backed up onto the empty street, watching the house as he did. He looked at the fresh paint and the mowed lawn and the porch swing. He turned out onto the street and shifted from reverse, then drove up along the street, American flags on lawns, lights and television sets visible in the windows.

He didn't really have anywhere to go. It had been this way since he got back. He was going to go down to Tucker's and get drunk and then he was going to come home and park crooked in the driveway and fall asleep on the couch. If he was lucky, he'd get some skin along the way.

PART I

THE QUIET AMERICAN

Chapter 1

In the distance, black hills stretched across the sky. The sky was grey and stark. It swam with shifting clouds. Before the black hills were rolling hills of green, which sloped up towards the sky, dotted white with sheep.

Sparse farmhouses lay across the landscape, separated by hedgerows and stone walls. Occasionally, a thin road wound its way, like a tendril, across the earth. Ray sat back in the seat with his arm on the windowsill.

In Ireland, everything was smaller, tighter. Trees were short and dense; undergrowth, thick and tangled. Stretches of contorted bramble intersected pristine pastures. Though less vast, it was somehow wilder than the country at home. It was a matter of constraints, of concentration.

But he wasn't a country man. He grew up in the city. He knew dockyards and project housing, university dorms and campus greens, and the cold and sterile halls of federal buildings. The wilds at home were as foreign to him as Palestine. More so, even.

The train slowed. Ray tried to tune out the ever-present vibration and rattle. To focus on it entirely was overwhelming. An isolated platform emerged, drawing around the train suddenly: a low stone wall, a concrete platform.

The sign on the platform said Collooney - *Cúil Mhuine*. The English and the Irish. He watched people on the platform outside the train. He made an effort to look casual and bored. Really, he watched with care. He watched other single men around his age—late twenties, early thirties.

A strongly built man in a wool jumper and peaked cap entering the carriage at the front drew his attention. The man stepped in and began to make his way down the center of the aisle, eyeing the people in their seats as he passed. The man had a thick black beard and no hair beneath the cap. Raymond had never seen him before but he looked familiar, and familiarity alone was enough to take notice of.

The man had the calm hard face and cold eyes of someone who didn't falter, but it was the harsh north-west of Ireland and that in itself wasn't rare. Raymond leaned back further in the seat and tilted his head to look out the window once more. He watched a blonde woman on the platform and let his eyes wander. In the reflection on the glass, he saw the bearded man take a seat a few rows up and then turned his eyes back away from the window as the train pulled out of the station.

Ireland was a place that his parents referred to as *home* when he was a boy but a place that he felt little relation to. To him, Ireland suggested stories of trouble and hardship, and a myth that bound together neighborhoods in America. He'd always heard of people touching down on the shores with a newfound sense of purpose and fulfilment. When he touched down, he felt nothing. The grass was green and Dublin, like most cities, was a shithole.

Coming out west by train, he saw the country for what it really was. The lands were tightly packed and everything enclosed. It was no wonder violence unfolded with such totality here. Roots ran deep and were tangled. The fields and pastures might stretch out but, eventually, hills or hedgerows would encircle. If it wasn't a hill or mountain or hedge or forest, it was the sea and that was definite. There were borders everywhere.

He was here because of borders. The border on the island, the south and the North. The other border, the one that concerned him, the East and the West.

What mattered about that border to him was how it impacted their own—the border between the Soviet Bloc and the Free World. In this war, you had to pick a side. The little countries and their conflicts swayed the pendulum: the Vietnams, the Cubas, the Irelands.

The problem was that borders were never as clear as you'd like, Raymond thought. He watched the fields grow up along the tracks again, the little Irish cattle moving between grazing grounds. Americans were allies of the British, but they were also friends of the Irish. He had cousins who sent their life savings to the Republican Cause, and so did everyone in Washington. He had come here to put American guns into Irish hands so that the Soviets didn't get there first. If the Soviets co-opted the revolution, Europe would be under siege. But those guns would inevitably be used against the British, their greatest allies in Europe. It was a complex world.

The train began to slow again as it neared Sligo town. The fields and hills were swallowed up by a stretch of industrial buildings, cement blocks, and warehouses. Chain-link fences ran along parking lots filled with trucks and rusty red shipping containers draped with fishing net. There was something familiar in the scene, like the outskirts of any city he'd ever been to. There was something unfamiliar in it too. Somehow, the walls were poured differently than in America.

To the west, behind the industrial stretch, a swell of dark brown and green earth stood out against the sky like a massive tree stump with a bulge on top like an anthill. Behind that, the sky. The stone walls along the platform blocked out the rest of the world as the train slowed. It came to a stop. Around him, people began to move toward the exits, pulling wheeled suitcases and carrying bags down the aisle.

Sligo was the end of the line so he waited in his seat as men and women departed the train around him. He was in no hurry. He watched the bearded man in the peaked cap stand through the gap in the seats. Once he left the train, Raymond stood. He grabbed his leather jacket from the seat beside him and his canvas duffel and began to walk up the aisle to the end of the carriage. The other man got off and disappeared into the crowd.

Raymond stepped out onto the platform. A damp mist hung in the air like rain aching to fall. He looked around the platform. The man had already gone through the station. There had been no one else on board that drew his attention, though he kept an eye on lingering passengers in any case. He wandered down the platform. When he reached the doors, he passed through into the lobby of the train station.

The train station was an old stone building. Smooth cream-colored tiles stretched across the short distance to the exit. He walked across the floor to the exit and passed through the station without paying much heed to those inside. So far, no one knew that he was in Ireland but his handler back home. It was unlikely that he would be identified already. He had not made contact with the embassy in Dublin because he needed to keep a low profile to avoid alerting the authorities of his presence. Key to that was absolute discretion. He would act alone. Contact with the Company would be almost non-existent.

Americans believed that the Irish had a culture of silence. On the streets of Boston, people prided themselves on Irish blood because it meant they wouldn't talk. The truth, Ireland

14

was lousy with rats. As he'd been shown, British authorities infiltrated the IRA to the highest levels. Because of that, no one could know where he really stood. As far as he was concerned now, he was not a CIA operative in Ireland but an Irish American gunrunner with a romantic attachment to the Cause. This facade alone would keep him alive, Britain friendly, and the Western bloc stable.

He stepped back out into the fresh misty air on the other side of the station. The bearded man was nowhere in sight. The train station sat at the top of an incline above the road. The Great Southern Hotel to the right, sitting prominently on a stretch of land. It looked like a colonial building in Havana more than a hotel in a European town. It had tall flat cream walls, small rectangular windows, and a large prominent staircase leading up to the entryway.

Raymond slung the duffel over his shoulder and walked down the staircase from the station to the narrow street below. Along both sides nearly identical rows of attached stone buildings ran the length of the street: storefronts, pubs, and houses. He looked down at his watch and checked the time. He was to meet his contact in Sligo, an American gunrunner named Tommy Slowey, at a quarter after three in O'Neil's Pub along the river. He'd been shown a picture of the man. He still had fifteen minutes. Slowey moved in dangerous circles and looked out for his own. He also controlled this end of a smuggling operation from the other side.

He walked down the street to the center of town. European cars rolled up and down the narrow road beside him, working their way through the congested intersection. He waited for a gap in the traffic and hurried across the street, following it further still along Wine Street. When he crossed through the intersection, the buildings got a little taller but otherwise nothing changed.

Despite the mist, he felt the freshness of the sea not far off. Small puddles gathered in dips along the sidewalk, which was barely wide enough for two to cross paths without bumping shoulders. A woman a little further along pushed a baby in a stroller. A few men stood against a corner ahead smoking and watching women. The buildings along the street were all interconnected. The façades differed depending on the tenant. There were pubs, newsstands, cafés, and clothing stores.

He continued past a post office and a bank and a few winding streets that turned off, revealing hotels and pubs. He reached a bridge passing over a river and crossed to the other side of the street. A path ran along the river, turning into a cobblestone street which ran with the water, curving gently with the flow. Raymond reached into his pocket and pulled out a slip of paper. He checked the address on it and then continued walking. To his left, water rolled under the stone bridge, swirling and sloshing.

It was growing colder. Raymond stopped at a stone bench beside the railing overlooking the river and set his bag down. He slipped his leather jacket on, picked the bag back up, and continued on toward the pub on the corner.

Chapter 2

Tommy Slowey sat at the bar with a cigarette between his fingers and a pint of Guinness in his hand. He was skinny. The bones of his wrist looked ready to burst through the pasty skin around them. The blue linen shirt he wore draped over his shoulders without shape. As soon as he opened the door and stepped into O'Neil's, Raymond could see Slowey's little blue eyes on him in the mirror behind the bar.

O'Neil's was a classic Irish bar, filled with nooks and crannies in which men could all but disappear at any time of day. Raymond walked up to the bar and leaned on it a few feet away from the American. "Been to the races?" he asked, glancing over.

"Not since Sunday," Slowey replied. He tapped the cigarette in the ashtray and stood up slowly. He held his Guinness steady in his right hand, letting the smoke trail up along the rim of the glass. He took his brown coat off the back of the stool and then moved down to a little booth near the back of the room.

The bartender came up to Raymond, cleaning a glass with a rag. He glanced at the bag but said nothing. "Just a pint," Raymond said. The barman nodded and brought the glass over to the taps. He tilted the glass and filled it three-quarters of the way, then set it down on the bar.

"Twenty-five pence," he said. Raymond reached into his pocket and pulled out a few coins. He looked at them, then paid. He leaned on the bar and looked over to the booth where Slowey sat. The man took the money. He let the pint settle, then filled it the rest of the way and set it down in front of Raymond.

Raymond took it and walked across the pub to the table at the back. He unslung the duffel bag from his shoulder and dropped it on the floor beneath the table, then sat down in the booth across from the gunrunner. He set the Guinness down on a coaster on the hard oak.

"*Sláinte*," Slowey said, raising his glass.

"*Sláinte.*"

Slowey took a long drink, then set the glass down. "So, you're the guy," he said, examining Raymond.

Raymond didn't respond.

"Who do you work for?" Slowey asked.

Again, Raymond didn't reply. He examined the man instead. Slowey had thin black hair combed back over his scalp. His pronounced brow cast a perpetual shadow over his eyes, which looked smaller than any Raymond had seen before. The top three buttons on his shirt were undone revealing a greasy looking patch of tangled black hair.

"I don't care who you work for," Slowey said eventually, before tilting the Guinness to his lips. He set it down on the table and then wiped the foam from his thin lips with the back of his hand. "All I care is that you want what I want."

"And what do you want?" Raymond asked.

"To make money," Slowey said. His lips curled up around his yellowing teeth in a crooked grin.

"Then we're out for the same," Raymond said. "Why else would I be here?"

Slowey tilted his head and looked back up at the bar. He looked back at Raymond and leaned in. "Come on," he said. "Who do you work for? You can tell me."

"How long have you been over?" Raymond asked, though he knew the answer already.

Slowey shook his head. He looked disgusted. "How can I trust you if I don't even know who you work for?" he asked. "Bucky said New York. Westies, is it?"

Raymond began to shift toward the edge of the booth, ready to leave. Slowey's left hand shot out and grasped him by the wrist, clutching him tight with surprising strength. His hand was cold and clammy. "Don't touch me," Raymond said.

Slowey eased his grasp. "Alright," he said. "I won't ask again." He let go entirely and leaned back again. "It's someone big though," he said, grinning. "Bigger than Southies, eh?"

Raymond glanced around the bar. No one else paid them any heed. He leaned against the back of the booth again. He would have to be careful with Slowey. "How long have you been here?" he asked for a second time.

"Three years," Slowey said, his voice raspy and hoarse. He leaned away from Raymond and coughed into his fist, then cleared his throat. He reached into his chest pocket and pulled out a pack of cigarettes.

He'd told the truth so far, Raymond thought. "Why'd you come over?"

Slowey lit his cigarette and dropped the lighter on the table. "Everybody's dream, isn't it?"

The door opened and Raymond looked over. An older man came in and took a seat at the bar. By the time he sat down, the bartender was already pouring his pint.

"We needed someone on this end," Slowey said.

Raymond looked back at him and nodded. "And you set up a line."

"I did," Slowey said. "And it ran smoothly for two years. Didn't lose a single shipment."

"How did you avoid the police?"

"Gardaí are the same as any other cops," Slowey said.

"And the Brits?"

"Slow down," Slowey said, grinning again, flashing his yellow teeth. "You won't get my panties off before you've bought me dinner." He drew on the cigarette and then blew the smoke across the table. "Why don't you," he said, pointing with his cigarette, "tell me, what the fuck it is you think you're going to do here?"

"We're going to re-establish the line," Raymond said, leaning on the table.

"You and your mystery men back home," Slowey said.

"That's right."

"And my part is?"

"The gracious host," Raymond said.

Slowey gave a wheezing cackle, spit out in a single burst. He tapped the cigarette, dropping ash to the tray. Then his face turned cold in an instant. His eyes were dark. "I don't exactly know why Bucky wanted to bring you boys on but it feels a lot like muscling in."

"It's not muscling if we play nice," Raymond said. "Let's not start off on the wrong foot here."

Slowey eyed him and dropped the butt of the cigarette into the tray. He took another drink.

"Bucky had supply shortages and you lost your in on this side. Let's be honest, you had a good thing going when it was going but now it's gone."

"Fucking prod fucks," Slowey muttered.

Raymond glanced over his shoulder and then leaned in closer. "What happened?"

Slowey shook his head. "The fella I dealt with got nabbed crossing the border and ended up in the Maze. One of the quartermasters made contact but before anything happened he got wiped out by a fucking car bomb."

"And there was no one else?"

"The communication fell apart," Slowey said.

"And that ended it?"

"I made contact with a man here in Sligo. That's why I come up. They've started to move toward this system where you only know members of your own cell, on account of all the rats. I've got an in with the Sligo Brigade. But, like you said," Slowey added, "Bucky run into problems with supply. Something with his contact on the base."

"That's where I come in," Raymond said, leaning back. "We've got the supply. And we'll never run out."

"Where are you getting them?"

"Ah, you'll have to buy me dinner first," Raymond said, grinning. "Look, if we get this going again, there's enough money in it for everyone."

"And of course, there's the Cause," Slowey said.

"Of course, there's the Cause." Raymond smiled.

Slowey laughed. He picked up the packet and took out another cigarette. He tapped it on the table and turned it between his fingers. "Alright," he said. "I see the way the cards are falling. And Bucky says jump, so I jump." He tucked the cigarette between his lips and picked up the lighter. He held it to the flame and drew. When it caught, he took it out and let the smoke release. "So, you want an introduction to my friend."

"I do."

Slowey nodded and stared at the glass on the table in front of him, contemplating. "Another round?"

Raymond looked at his half-empty glass. Then he drained it. "Another round," he said, setting it down on the table, foam slowly running down the side.

"Right then. This one's yours."

Chapter 3

A red double door, on an innocuous looking front, sat between a small restaurant and a pub. Raymond brought the key to the lock and opened it. He stepped into a narrow entryway with a twenty-foot ceiling. Slowey had already spoken with Bucky—that was clear. He was just flexing, making sure that Ray knew where he stood.

There were a few metal mailboxes on the wall to his left and an even narrower set of stairs led up to a rectangle of light above. He let the door close behind him and began to walk up the metal stairs. He'd had a few more at the pub and felt a little unsteady on his feet.

The stairs led him up to the second story and brought him out onto the roof of the restaurant below, a courtyard above the street. Four buildings stretched up like townhouses from the courtyard, each with rose-colored sand and cement walls, separate doorways, and external windows.

His unit was to the right. He walked to it and opened the door, stepping inside. Another set of stairs led him up to a small second floor landing, where there were two doors. Raymond slipped the key into the lock on number 11 and opened the door.

The flat was small and clean. He closed the door behind him. He saw the bathroom directly to his left. He went down the hall and through the doorway on the right, entering a rectangular living room and kitchen. Ray wondered how much Bucky knew himself, if he'd been told that he was being used or if he'd simply been duped as well. Either way, it didn't really matter.

Linoleum tile and synthetic wood flooring marked the division. There were three large windows against the external wall. The room was modestly furnished. A typewriter stood on a desk in the corner with a stack of blank paper beside it. He'd write reports there in code and mail them to a false address in London. He'd receive coded responses in a tabloid newspaper

He set the duffel bag down beside the door and crossed to the nearest window. It looked over a narrow alleyway to an identical set up on the other side. A second-story courtyard and a series of rose units. At street level, he could see stone facades and a pub below.

A row of kegs sat in a puddle on the cobblestone near the back door of yet another pub, which must have been located on the main street. The grey sky grew darker. Seagulls perched on the black shingles of the roof across from him. A slight rain began to fall, pattering against the glass.

A light came on in a window across the alleyway, revealing a sheer white curtain tied by a red string at the edge. A woman with tangled black hair came into view in her living room, entirely oblivious to his presence. She was in her mid-thirties, a few years older than he was. She lifted a blanket from a green sofa and folded it, then draped it across the back. He felt like a voyeur but that was nothing new. He watched her move around the flat for a while and then turned away from the window.

Raymond crossed to a small wooden cabinet beside the oven and stooped down. He opened it. It was empty other than a half-empty bag of rice and an open box of Corn Flakes. He took the cereal box out and stood up, setting it on the laminate countertop. He opened the top of the box and looked inside. It was half-full. Raymond reached into the box, plunging his hand into the cereal. He searched through it until he found what he was looking for and grabbed it with his fingers. He pulled out a small paper bag and shook the loose flakes from it. Then he unfolded the bag and dumped it on the countertop. Inside was a fold of bank notes. *Saorstát*, Irish pounds.

He closed the cereal box and put it back in the cupboard. He swept flakes off the table, then picked up the money and flicked through it. There was a lot. He peeled off a few notes and tucked them into the pocket of his jeans. He brought the rest of the fold over to his duffel bag and tucked it into the pocket of a shirt inside. He walked to one of the other windows, parted the curtain, and looked down to the narrow alley below. Moss grew in tufts on the roofs. Voices of drunken young men laughing and yelling at girls carried up to him, echoing between the walls.

Raymond turned away from the window. He picked up the duffel bag and went down the hall to the bedroom. It was a small, square room with a double bed and a wardrobe. A window looked out over the courtyard below. He dropped the bag on the bed and sat down beside it. He thought over the events of the afternoon. He'd arrived in Sligo just hours before and he'd already met with Slowey, the gunrunner, and was set up to be introduced to a member of the IRA. Things were moving quickly.

But he knew better than to get ahead of himself. Things could go perfectly for months and then one minor slip up, a matter of seconds, could bring it all crashing down. The most important thing was that no one could know who he really was. This was a lion's den. He knew for a fact that the KGB had a man in Ireland, though he didn't know where. If he was lucky, the agent was at the embassy in Dublin. If he was unlucky, they had already infiltrated the organization.

Raymond stood up and walked to the window. He watched as rain fell to the courtyard from the dark sky above. It was a little country but its wars were far larger. The battlefield larger than they could ever know. It was growing late. He turned away from the window and walked out into the hall. He went down the hall to the door, grabbing his leather jacket from the peg along the way, and left the flat. The flat door echoed in the landing.

The sound of his footsteps down the stairs was like rain on the tin roofs across the way. When he reached the courtyard, the air was cold and fresh. Droplets splattered on his shoulders and head, but they were small and did not faze him much. A young man with long, curling black hair and a thin mustache came through the courtyard from another unit. He wore blue jeans and a denim jacket with a checkered shirt beneath. Raymond nodded to him and watched him go.

He crossed the courtyard and took the stairs down to the street level. He went out the doors and found himself standing back on the cobblestone along the river with the indigo blue light trying to work through the clouds. The rain was still falling. The wet ground caught slivers of light. He wandered up to the metal railing across from the entrance to his building and leaned on the slick metal, looking down to the flowing water.

The river was not wide at this point. The water moved slowly but with force, curling and rippling. To his right, it flowed beneath a stone bridge that cars occasionally rolled over, headlights shaking along the road. To the left, it turned up beneath another bridge. Across from him was a small carpark with three cars in the lot, each a slight variation of the same model.

In the shadow of the bridge, he saw a heron on the rocks. It stood still, staring at something in the distance, its long neck curled into an *s*, grey feathers like hair. It took a step, extending its long legs, and took flight. The heron was a majestic, awkward animal. It flew with a lumbering gait. Each slow thrust of its wings allowed it to soar for incredible distance. It was something prehistoric, he thought, out of place in this modern world. Yet, it carried itself with pride.

Raymond turned and moved away from the railing. He walked toward the center of town. He was already gaining Tommy Slowey's trust. Slowey was a lifelong crook from South Boston, born in 1939. In those days, an Irish boy in South Boston became a cop, a crook, or a factory worker, and the cards were dealt at an early age. Slowey caught his first case at thirteen—armed robbery. That set the course.

Down a narrow street to his left, Raymond saw the red and yellow lights of a chipper. The scent of vinegar and frying oil wafted through the mist. He'd boarded the train in Dublin that morning with a coffee and scone and hadn't eaten since. He needed something and didn't really care what it was. He turned up the alleyway. It was Italian. Antonio's. Back home, Italians did pizza and pasta. Here it was fish and chips.

A bell rang out when he opened the glass door. There were half a dozen people inside. By the way they looked at him, he felt like they could already tell that he didn't belong. It was a feeling he got used to fast. The three women, two men, and young boy all looked like they knew one another. A bald little Italian man stood behind the counter with an apron tied around his stomach. A green, white, and red flag was painted on the wall.

"Next!" the Italian yelled, staring directly at Raymond.

Raymond walked up to the counter. "Fish and chips," he said.

The man behind the counter nodded. "Forty p."

Raymond paid him. He took a step back and leaned on a red ledge along the edge of the shop and looked back at the glass front. It was dark out, he could barely see through. He saw the reflection of everyone else inside. They were still quiet, watching him. He tried to appear as if he was not paying them any attention, that he did not notice their unease. Slowly, their interest waned. Conversation sparked. He faded.

After a few moments, the Italian set damp brown paper bags on the countertop. They were collected by the women, who then disappeared with the rattle of the bell. The boy got his chips next. He hurried past Raymond with his fingers in the bag and the smell of vinegar in the air.

The men were next, and then Raymond was alone. He stood in the chipper looking at second-rate photographs of Italy. The sun and the color and the ocean always in view or at least within reach of imagination.

A newspaper was thrown down on the counter and the grease left a mark. He picked it up, nodded to the man, and sat at the little red countertop in the corner near the window.

The rain still fell against the glass, but it was even more gentle than it had been before. He heard the slow patter of the droplets as he doused the cod in tartar sauce and shook malt vinegar on the chips. The white fish was flaky beneath the beer batter. The chips were thick and crisp. He ate alone and thought of home, or what he had of one.

Then the bell rattled and a woman walked in. She was younger than him, a student, maybe. He watched her in the reflection on the glass. She wore a heavy green sweater and flared trousers. Her brown hair was long and straight and had a red hue in the light. She wore thick glasses with wide lenses. She glanced at him and then went up to the counter.

"Ms. Kelly!" the Italian shouted, beaming. "Chips on the way!"

"Hi Antonio," she said with a laugh.

"Don't you worry," Antonio said. "They'll be just a moment."

"Thanks a million." She turned and leaned back against the counter and looked back up at Raymond, the only other person in the shop. He smiled and went back to his food. He finished eating as Antonio handed the chips across the counter. She thanked Antonio again and turned to leave.

Raymond stood up and cast his basket into the bin. He ran his hand through his long black hair and glanced back at the woman. She was looking his way again and they made eye contact for a brief moment. Her eyes were green beneath the glasses. He allowed himself to share the fleeting glance. He made the most of such glances when he could. It was a moment of connection in a life where that was not often possible.

She was looking at him like she knew him or intended to try. He turned and went back out through the door and into the gentle rain, letting the bell ring behind him. He looked up and down the street, then headed back the way he'd come.

Chapter 4

Raymond opened the door to O'Neil's and stepped inside. It was dark. There was oak and glass and warped mirrors with liquor ads. Three men sat alone inside.

Tommy Slowey leaned on the bar with an ashtray and a pint. He finished it and ordered another round. Raymond took the stool beside him. The barman poured two and let them set.

"How are you finding Sligo?" Slowey asked.

"It's fine," Raymond said.

"Got your crib?"

"Yeah. Just down the road."

"Nice place?"

"It'll do for now," Raymond said. He thanked the barman when the Guinness was placed before him. "Your friend on the way?" he asked, looking at Slowey when they were alone again.

"No," Slowey said. "We'll go to him."

Raymond nodded. He lifted the glass and took a drink. It was smooth and full. He set it down and watched another man a little further down the bar pick at a scab on the back of his hand. It started to bleed and he pulled a handkerchief from his pocket to dab at the blood.

"Where'd you grow up?" Slowey asked. He brushed something from his shoulder and then patted down the few loose strands on top of his head.

"Buffalo," Raymond said.

"You work with the family?"

Raymond shook his head. "These days that's a sure way to a RICO case."

"I grew up in Boston," Slowey said. He turned and looked at Raymond as he spoke, peering at him through beady eyes.

"Southie."

"Through and through."

"How many generations?"

"I don't know," Slowey said. "South Boston is forever, far as I care."

"You care much about the Irish stuff?"

Slowey shrugged. "I thought I was Irish 'til I came here. Now, I don't know. All I know is my neighborhood."

"You don't feel at home here?"

Slowey shook his head. "The tenements are home. There's no escaping that."

"What do you do around here?"

"You're looking at it. There's a bookie two doors down."

They finished their drinks and stepped outside. The sun shone overhead and the skies were blue. Two men sat on a stone bench beside the river watching the birds. One of the men wore a wide-brimmed hat and a tweed jacket. The other had a blue flat cap on his head and a wool sweater. Both smoked cigarettes.

Slowey reached into his chest pocket and pulled out his own pack. He tapped a cigarette out and set it between his lips. He offered one to Raymond, who shook his head. Slowey lingered in the shadows of the doorway and lit the cigarette, then tucked the pack back into his pocket. It sat in the linen, hanging off his chest a little to the left of the heart.

"Gerry's going to meet us down near the harbour," Slowey said.

"Is that where the boats come in?" Raymond asked.

"No. It's where he works."

"You know this guy well?"

Slowey smiled, revealing his crooked yellow teeth. "Better than I know you."

"Fair enough."

Slowey stepped away from the pub and led the way down along the river. They walked up past the old men and through a laneway to another street. "I've a car parked up here," Slowey said. "Just a little further on." He led the way to another laneway and up into a parking lot half-full of cars. He went over to a red Citroën GS and took out his keys. "I don't drive much so I leave it here most of the time."

Raymond nodded and leaned on the roof. Slowey unlocked the door and got in. Raymond opened the door and climbed into the passenger side, lowering himself onto the beige fabric seat and pulling the door after him. It clapped and echoed. The car was low and felt like it was sagging. It smelled like stale cigarettes.

Slowey turned the key in the ignition and the engine struggled to turn over. Eventually it did and the car roared to life. "She's testy but gets the job done," he said.

The Citroën rolled across the uneven tarmac of the parking lot, rattling and jostling in the bumps. It was steady but felt unstable. The frame moved more than it should have on the suspension. Slowey guided the car down the slope and out onto the road below. The front bumper scraped the ground. The sound was grating and raw.

Slowey turned left up the road and began to drive down the narrow little street toward the water. There were a few other cars parked along the edge. There was hardly enough room for the Citroën to pass. Raymond watched people on the street. It was quiet. There were a few tall, slim houses with chipped fronts and crumbling steps. He saw children peering out through the darkened glass. Mothers hung wet clothes on lines across the tiny squares of uncut grass before the houses. They drove along the water, past warehouses and walls.

Gerry Cooney was leaning against the chain-link fence in a black denim jacket, a tattered pair of Levi's, and Doc Martens when they drove up. The crooked links behind him sagged beneath the weight. Barbed wire ran along the top. He was a slender man but had large shoulders and something in his eyes gave the impression of strength. He was only about twenty-five years old.

Slowey pulled over at the side of the road across from the yard that Gerry stood in front of. He parked beside another fence, where a lot of fishing boats were sitting up out of the water. He turned off the ignition and opened the car door to step out. Raymond followed suit. They crossed over the black road to the fence on the other side.

"Gerry," Slowey said.

"What's the story?"

"This is Ray."

"You're over from the States?" Gerry asked, looking Raymond up and down.

"I am."

"You in long?"

"Arrived in Dublin yesterday."

Gerry nodded. "How long are you over?"

Raymond shrugged. "I'm not sure. A while yet."

"Let's go for a drive," Slowey said. Gerry moved off the fence, letting the loose wire ease with the release of pressure. Slowey turned and glanced up the road before crossing back over to the car. Raymond followed close behind him. Slowey got in the car first. Raymond went around the hood and opened the back door.

"Stay up front," Gerry said. "I'll take the back." As he spoke, he opened the back door on the passenger side and climbed in.

Raymond took the front without hesitation, though he felt it inside. He didn't like having the stranger sitting behind him, out of sight, but he also knew that he could not show weakness in front of these men. "Where are we going?" he asked, looking over at Slowey.

Slowey turned the key in the ignition and let the engine turn over. "Just a little drive," he said. He pulled out onto the road and continued further. Behind the fences were fishing boats and nets. There were shipping containers, crates, and a junkyard. Then they moved a little further along and the fence hiding the water fell away and the water stretched out behind a small stone wall, flat and still. Beyond it were rolling black mountains against the grey sky.

The car moved into the shadows of tangled, dense foliage. The road was little wider than the car—about the width of a tractor. On one side, a once manicured hedgerow separated the road from a grazing field. There were no cattle or sheep in it.

On the other side, a beaten down hedge merged with a line of trees, shrubs, ferns, and mosses. The wall of vegetation stretched up above them so all that Raymond could see was twisted limbs, branches, and growth.

Slowey turned the radio on. John Lennon came on: "Whatever Gets You Thru the Night." Raymond let the window down and the air was fresh and cool. He began to feel more at ease. The Citroën turned at the curve of the road and led them out further along the coast.

The hedges and trees disappeared and it was a clear view down to the sea. The grass was lush, green. A sandy beach stretched out below. The grey cover cleared and the sun crept through with a wash of baby blue. Cormorants gathered in the water, stretching their necks.

The hard curve of a pistol pressed into Raymond's head, just behind the ear. He could feel the cold metal on the skin. In the rear-view mirror, he saw Gerry Cooney's arm. The handgun was small and black, a Browning, maybe. The pressure of the barrel sent a wave of pain through the back of his skull. His legs and jaw tensed instinctively.

"What the fuck is this?" Raymond asked. He did not dare move his head.

"Don't talk," Gerry said.

"Tommy—"

"Shut the fuck up," Gerry said.

Slowey didn't answer Raymond. He glanced over at him from the corner of his eye. Slowey tapped his cigarette out the open window and then tucked it back between his lips. The cloud cover closed again and the world fell dark and grey.

Slowey slowed the car and turned down onto an even narrower lane, which led down toward the black sea. They passed metal fences leading into fields. It was quiet. They were no more than fifteen minutes from town but it seemed empty.

He slowed the car at the side of the road beside a muddy drive leading up to a metal barn. A half-collapsed stone cottage sat in the muck. It had no windows or doors and was missing half its roof. The half that remained was collapsing. "Who are you?" Gerry asked.

"Raymond Daly."

"I said who the fuck are you?" The barrel pressed harder into the back of his head.

"Raymond Daly. I came from America. Didn't Tommy—"

"Tommy doesn't know you," Gerry said.

"I think there's been a misunderstanding," Raymond said. "Put the gun down."

"You think you can come over from America and play around with the fuckin' IRA? You don't know a thing about it. This isn't a game," Gerry said. His tone was cold. "This is history. This is our lives."

"I know," Raymond said. He stared into the rear-view mirror, examining the man's face, trying to assess whether or not he really had it in him to pull the trigger. "Tommy, tell him...."

Tommy Slowey looked across at him from the driver's seat. He leaned on the steering wheel, dangling his arms over it with the cigarette in hand. His brow was damp with sweat. It looked thick and greasy. "Tell him who you are," Slowey said.

"Ask Bucky," Raymond said.

"Bucky ain't here," Slowey said. "I'm here. And Gerry's here."

"Who do you work for?" Gerry asked.

"The name won't mean a thing to you," Raymond said slowly.

"Give it to us anyway."

"Jimmy Barry in New York. We're working with the same people as Tommy."

"What do you want with us?"

"We want to bring guns in from the other side. Like I told Tommy and Tommy told you."

Gerry leaned in closer. He dragged the gun down into the soft flesh beneath Raymond's ear lobe and pressed it in hard. "You an informer?"

"No," Raymond said.

His hot breath bathed Raymond's neck. "I so much as smell a rasher on you I'm going to put a bullet in your head and leave you in that field," Gerry said.

"I understand."

"What do you care about giving guns to the IRA?"

"I'm Irish," Raymond said. "My grandparents came from Cork."

"Everybody's fuckin' granny's from fuckin' Cork," Gerry said. "Try again."

"It's not philanthropy."

"We don't have the money to buy guns at the moment." Gerry said, pulling the handgun back. He rested the barrel across his lap.

Raymond exhaled slowly. "You don't have to pay a dime," he said. "There's a man in Brooklyn financing. Irish. You'd know his name. All you have to do is take the load." As he spoke, he saw that Gerry already knew that too.

"Have you spoken to this man in Brooklyn, Tommy?"

Slowey shook his head. "No," he said, "but Bucky says it's legit, so it's legit." He drew on the cigarette and blew the sharp wispy smoke across the car.

Gerry was rubbing the gun on his thigh, looking closely at Raymond between the seats. "So, it's all set up on the other side."

"It is," Raymond said.

"Where are the guns coming from?"

Raymond cleared his throat. "It's the same deal Tommy had going. We have a supplier on the other end. Guns are delivered, no questions asked. If you aren't interested, I'm sure others would be."

"You've not been in this country long enough to start burning bridges," Gerry said. He reached over the seat and tapped Slowey on the chest with the side of the pistol. "Alright, Tommy, take us back to town."

Slowey nodded and started the engine.

Chapter 5

Slowey turned the car around at a cattle gate and drove the winding road back to Sligo. The rain began to fall as they drove, pattering gently on the windshield and roof. The pock-marked road was slick and black. He slowed the car along the harbour and came to a stop in the same place they'd picked Gerry up.

Gerry tucked the gun in his waistband and pulled the leather jacket over it. "Bring him around tomorrow. Half two," he said.

"Callaghan's?" Slowey asked.

"Yeah," Gerry said. He opened the back door and got out of the car. As soon as it shut, Slowey pulled away from the curb.

Raymond watched Gerry in the rear-view mirror until he disappeared when the car turned left at the next intersection. "So, what does that mean?" he asked.

"It means you're meeting again," Slowey said.

"That good?"

"If it was bad, I'd be driving back alone."

"You set me up, Tommy."

Slowey reached over and turned on the radio. Van Morrison came on and he changed the station. *O'Doherty was taken from her home in Enniskillen on Monday morning. Her body was found on the side of the road ...*

Droplets beat across the windshield. The wipers cast a spray of water from the glass. "Does most of that stay in the North?" Raymond asked.

"The IRA have a policy not to do violence in the Republic." Slowey steered. "Sometimes it spills over. Or festers." The *F* was long and slithered from his lips.

"Killings?"

"Killings. Disappearances. The occasional bomb. Mostly near the border." Slowey pulled the car into the lot and guided it into a space, then shut off the engine. "There was a car bomb in Blacklion, over in Cavan, not long ago."

"What happened?"

"Three boys in balaclavas and British uniforms jacked a car, put a bomb in it."

"Were they soldiers?"

Slowey shrugged. "Paid or unpaid."

"Was anyone killed?"

He shook his head. "They forced the driver to park up in the middle of the village somewhere but he got word to the police before the thing went off. Evacuated the whole fuckin' town. They say it'd have blown the whole fuckin' village to pieces. No exaggeration."

"When was that?"

"Weeks, months ... I don't fuckin' know. Recent enough," he said. "You heard about them bombs in Dublin and Monaghan, yeah?"

Raymond watched the rain slide along the windshield. He had heard about them. He knew more than Slowey, likely. It was news in his world. Three bombs in Dublin within four minutes and another in Monaghan an hour later. Thirty-three killed and three-hundred wounded. No one took responsibility. They said that MI5 was behind it. "Yeah," Raymond said. "Fucking tragic."

Slowey pulled the key from the ignition and looked across for a moment. "Do you want to get something to eat?" he asked. "I'm starving."

"Yeah," said Raymond. He opened the passenger door and stepped out of the car. The rain was fresh and cold. Slowey followed him out and they walked down to the street. Slowey turned to the left. Raymond followed him from there. Slowey seemed to have moved on from the ambush already.

"Chinese on the corner there," Slowey said.

"That'll do."

"Right then."

They walked down to the end of the block and crossed over to a Chinese restaurant called the Golden Dragon on the corner. It had a false front with wooden lettering. The woodwork was painted deep red and green. Gold trimmings adorned it. Slowey opened the door and the man behind the counter nodded to them without looking up from his newspaper.

The room was small and almost empty. Cheap decorations hung from the rafters. Paintings and screens hung on the walls. A young couple sat at the back of the restaurant arguing about something in hushed tones.

Slowey pulled out a metal chair and took a seat at a table near the front door. Raymond pulled out the chair across from him and sat down. He picked up the paper menu and looked at it. There were about eighty options on it.

"How well do you know Gerry?" Raymond asked.

"Not well," Slowey said. He lit a cigarette and leaned back in the metal chair, letting the legs rise up from the sticky tiled floor. There was no music playing and the whirring of a dusty fan in the corner was the only background noise.

The man came up to the table with a pen in his hand and the newspaper folded beneath his arm. He was small and thin.

He didn't speak. "Let me have the General Tso," Slowey said. "And a Coke."

"I'll do the satay chicken," Raymond said, flipping the menu absently in his hands. He dropped it on the table and looked up. "Just water." The man nodded and then wandered back toward the kitchen slowly, feet pattering across the tile floor.

"Like I said before, my man Kevin was interned," Slowey said, dropping the chair back onto the floor. "Ended up in the Maze. I've never done business with Gerry."

"How do you decide who to work with?" Raymond asked. He couldn't tell if Slowey had any kind of ideological commitments or if he was just a gangster with an Irish name.

"You work with who you can," Slowey said, tapping the cigarette on the ashtray. "Bucky put me in touch with someone when I came over and now I'm the man in the know," he said, raising his eyebrows. The waiter came back with a Coke and a glass of water and set them down. Slowey nodded to him. "That's the thing they don't get back home. You can't come over here and just look up the IRA. There're more factions in it than a high-school cheerleading squad."

"Factions?"

He blew smoke. "There's communists and everything. OIRA, PIRA, INLA … political bullshit. Family feuds." He reached up and ran his hand through his hair. "Even the fuckers themselves don't know who they're dealing with, except that it's their cousins and their brothers and their girlfriend's sister's husband."

Raymond looked out the window at an old woman pushing a shopping basket along the sidewalk. "Sounds messy."

"If they could stop going at one another they'd be far better off. They've got enough to worry about with the loyalists and the Brits and the police."

"Under siege in their own homes," Raymond said, quoting something he'd read in a dossier.

Slowey ignored him. "Rats are the real problem. No trust anymore." The waiter came back with their food and set it down on the table in front of them.

"Thanks," Raymond said. They ate in silence. When he was done, Raymond looked out the window. Gerry Cooney was walking down the other side of the street with a woman beside him. Raymond watched them without comment for a while. That was key: observation—reflection before reaction. After a moment, he recognized the woman as Ms. Kelly, the girl from the chip shop. "There's Gerry," he said.

Slowey looked up from his food. Sauce was dripping down his chin. He wiped his mouth with the back of his hand. "It's a small town."

"Who's that with him?"

Slowey squinted across the road and then shook his head. "That'd be Aoife," he said. "Cousin or something." He turned his attention to Raymond. "Word of advice, don't go there. You already escaped death once today."

He watched her walk until she disappeared from view. The sway of her hips. His mother would have loved for him to end up with a girl like that—a real colleen bawn, as she used to say, never without a sense of vitriol and envy. "How does it work on this end?" Raymond asked, looking back to Slowey, who was severing his chicken with the edge of his fork.

"What's that?"

"The shipments."

Slowey put down the fork. He looked over his shoulder and leaned closer. "That's my end," he said.

Raymond shook his head. "How's this supposed to work without trust?" he asked.

"Slow down, cowboy." Slowey grinned. "You've been here all of two days."

"And I've already had a gun in my ear."

"You came here with the intention of selling guns to the fucking IRA, Raymond. Tell me, what did you expect?"

The fan in the corner was rattling and the couple at the back of the restaurant got up to leave. Raymond eyed Slowey across the table. Slowey was scraping his knife and fork against the ceramic plate. He knew that he needed to ease up and let things take their course. Slowey was right. He'd only been in the country for two days.

This was only the second time he'd been out on his own. The first was in Laos, six months before. In Laos, it was different. Everyone knew who he was. Here, he was sitting across the table from a Southie hood in Sligo, pretending to be someone he wasn't. To him, it was uncharted territory. All the training in the world amounted to nothing if he couldn't keep his cool.

Slowey finished eating and dropped the knife and fork. He leaned back and let out a loud sigh. He reached his hand into the open shirt and scratched the tangle of hair on his chest, then ran his hand over the thin strands on his head and looked through the window at the people on the street, letting his beady eyes linger. He took his cigarettes from his chest pocket and lit one.

"Bum a smoke?" Raymond asked. Slowey tossed the pack across the table and he took one from it. He took the offered light and tried to look as natural as he could, then handed the pack back to Slowey. "Don't suppose there's somewhere you can catch a ball game around here?"

Slowey laughed. "Not a chance."

Chapter 6

There was a night in Laos that he couldn't forget. It was damp there too, only the dampness was hot. On the coast here, the sea took the thickness from the air and left it fresh. There, it was sticky and the air was thick. He had been in Laos to do the same thing he was doing here—courting guerillas. It was why they sent him.

Around him, the stone and brick and concrete were wet with rain. He leaned on the railing and looked down at the rolling water beneath the bridge. The water was nearly black because the sky above was grey with cloud. He felt the slight impact of the droplets on his shoulders and back, rattling off the leather skin. He could feel the envelope in the coat's inner pocket.

He thought about the cold feeling of the Browning barrel on the soft skin behind his ear. Some things were a matter of bravado but he had the sense that Gerry really would have pulled the trigger and left him dead at the side of the road and that Slowey would have let him do it.

A ragged-looking man pushed a bicycle along the road across the river. He could hear the squeak of the rusty wheels from where he stood. Behind the man, he saw the red wooden facade on the front of Callaghan's bar. That was where he'd been told to meet Gerry to discuss the guns. It wasn't neutral ground. They'd only discuss the matter where they felt safe.

Raymond straightened up and moved further along. There was a sharp smell in the air. He wondered if it was the river or something on the streets. He passed two old men who sat on the stone bench along the water smoking and feeding the birds.

"Ach, she was walking the boreen on the Monday and on the Wednesday they found her in the bog."

"'Tis a terrible thing."

"Isn't it just."

Their voices faded behind him and he turned up an alleyway to the left, cutting across the block. He wanted to familiarize himself with the town. He knew the maps and he'd seen surveillance photographs. On the ground, it was always different. He wandered the cobblestone until he stepped out on the next street over. He walked along Wine Street until he reached O'Connell. He stopped at the postbox and opened it. He glanced over his shoulder before he drew the envelope from his pocket and dropped it in the box—a coded report for Nelson.

He ran through the story in his head. He worked for Jimmy Barry in New York. Jimmy made a deal with Bucky, a South Boston crook who'd been running guns to the IRA. Bucky ran into issues with supply and Jimmy had no shortage of guns. They had private funding, an Irish American philanthropist. Bucky had a man on the ground but Jimmy wanted one too. It was as simple as that.

Ray walked until he found himself back at the front door of the building he was staying in. He unlocked the door and went up the stairs to the courtyard. He crossed it, watching the pigeons on the walls, and opened the second door. He took the stairs up to his flat and unlocked it, then stepped inside. The tile was solid beneath his feet.

The air in the flat was stale and humid. The room smelled like old laundry left to dry in a cold room. In the kitchen, he opened the fridge and stared at the empty shelves. The fridge felt barely colder than the air outside. He closed it and turned to the window. There were gulls on the roof across the alley.

He went into the living room and sat down on the sofa in front of the television. He picked up the remote from the small coffee table and turned it on. *Dad's Army* was on and he let it play for a while. He began to flick through the channels, brief glimpses of fictional worlds and ads. He stared at it and then shut it off again.

That night in Laos, he'd been scared. The air was thick and hot. It was taut. There was a boy in front of him that he didn't recognize and he spoke a language that Raymond didn't know. They were in an alleyway in the city and the dirty cement walls stretched up around them, covered in posters and revolutionary slogans in a foreign script. The ground beneath his feet was muck and dirt.

Everything was sticky. There were insects in the air and every time he tried to make a decision there was an insect in his ear or his eye or working its way down the back of his neck. He slapped them and itched and his fingernails were too short to do any good and he felt like he was going to cry from frustration and exhaustion. A camera lay on the ground at their feet.

The boy in front of them was thin and weak. He didn't fight back. A soldier held him against the wall by his dirty cotton shirt. The boy's eyes were wide with panic and pleading but his mouth kept slipping into a dirty yellow smirk. When it did, the amber lights above played across his teeth and Raymond could see the shadow of the insects crawling on them. It disgusted him. The soldier holding him looked to Raymond for direction.

If they let the boy go, he would tell what he knew and that mattered more than whether or not he intended to be a spy. Raymond meant to look away but the gun came up so fast he didn't have the chance. The shot was a dull slap and the boy's face tore. There was a hole like a star and blood and brain across the amber-lit wall. The soldier let go and the boy dropped to the ground, and then they continued to move.

Raymond stood up and walked through the kitchen to the window. It had two latches on the bottom and opened up at a slant like the wall of a tent. He unlatched it and cracked the window and the fresh air slipped in. Droplets pattered on the glass and ran down in small trickles. There was a seagull on the roof across the way that seemed to be watching him. He turned away from it.

He went to the fridge and opened it, staring at the empty shelves again. He closed it and sat down at the table. There was a restlessness that set in whenever life returned to its ordinary pace. When he was alone and the lies were gone and the tension was removed and the mission was peripheral. He stared at the swirling wood for a while and then stood up and closed the window. He took his jacket off the chair and slipped it on and went back out.

Outside, it was still wet and cool. He walked to the grocery store. He wandered the aisles absently, looking at the food on the shelves around him. The options were fewer than back home. It was simple, basic. He picked up some food: coffee, steak and potatoes, and milk and bread and eggs. He went back to the flat and put the steak and milk in the fridge. He set the bag on the table and looked around the flat. He turned on the radio on the counter in the corner of the kitchen. Gary Glitter was playing. He changed the station. There was news and sports results.

Ray turned off the radio and went back out. He walked up to Wine Street and wandered along it until he reached the Great Southern Hotel. He went up the wide colonial steps and glanced around the lobby as he walked through. The man behind the counter nodded to him as he entered. He took a stool at the bar and ordered a whiskey.

The room was almost empty. Two men near the door were drinking coffee. At the far end of the bar, a lone man sat with a pint in his hand. a young couple was sitting in a quiet corner where the light was low. Newlyweds, he thought. He heard a sense of excitement in their conversation. It had not yet faded to discontent or bitterness. He sipped the whiskey, warm and round and nutty, floral on the tail.

Barry White's rich waver seeped from the ceiling, settling comfortably. Raymond watched the sky outside begin to darken through the windows. The grey clouds seemed to grow lighter as it did, soaking up the white light of the moon. He thought of French hotels along the Mekong River, cream archways and white shutters, purple orchids on the windowsill. He took his jacket off and lay it across the stool beside him.

A woman came into the bar alone and ordered a gin. Raymond watched her. She took a seat and glanced around. She looked uncertain sitting alone. This was it, he thought. The chase. Like John Wayne breaking broncos on the Utah flats. It was the hunt and conquest that channeled, quelled, his restless energy. That exertion of total control, of gentle domination.

He unbuttoned the sleeves of his shirt and rolled them up, then waved the barman over.

"Another whiskey, sir?"

"Yes, please. And when that woman's glass is down to a third, send her another."

"Certainly."

He tilted the glass and finished his whiskey, then set the tumbler down before him. The barman poured him another and he paid for three drinks, told the man to keep the change. It was best to settle up in advance—to have the cards stacked in your favor from the very beginning. He lifted the glass. The nose was caramel and citrus. He let the aroma work, then took a drink. It was a touch, a hint. It washed the tongue. He felt the numb heat spread, carrying spice.

Barry White was no longer playing but the notes were soft and deep and lingered. He sat at an angle at the bar so he was looking past the woman to the door. He saw her head turn and adjusted his eyes. They met. The illusion of first contact. He let her feel that she'd been the cause—that he was no threat. He gave her a small smile and she didn't look away immediately. He did first.

He continued to drink at the bar. She was at a table along the wall. A bridge now existed. Eventually, the barman brought her another drink. He looked over and smiled, raised his glass. She looked uneasy for a moment and glanced at her glass. She was far enough into her own to feel it and not so deep that she could walk out and leave it.

She accepted the offered glass and nodded to him with a shy smile. He got down off the stool and picked up his jacket and wandered over to the table. "Mind if I join you?" he asked.

"No," she said. "Thank you," she added. She spoke with an Irish accent. He was glad.

Ray took a seat at the table across from her. "I hope I'm not imposing."

"Not at all. I was just having a quiet evening." She was still nursing her first drink.

"Are you staying in the hotel?" he asked.

"Yes. I'm only in town a few days."

"Business?"

"Yes," she said. "Are you staying at the hotel?"

"Yes."

She lit a cigarette and the smoke rose through the green light of the beer ad on the wall behind her. "You're American."

"I am."

"Whereabouts?"

"New York."

"I've always wanted to go."

"It's funny. Over there, everyone wants to come to Ireland." She smiled. "I don't know why. There's nothing here."

"There's history."

"Far too much."

The subtle cadence behind them was white noise—insulation. It kept their conversation between them alone. She was lonely and it made her amenable to him. She began her second drink. Raymond nursed his own with patience, allowing things to unfold. It was a series of exchanges. He made his play, advanced and circled. Deviations were corralled. It led, inevitably, to resignation—conquest.

They left the bar together and ascended the stairs.

Chapter 7

There were riots in the North. A soldier shot a twelve-year-old boy cutting through a hedgerow on his way home from school and when night fell petrol bombs began to shatter on land cruisers. Gunfire rattled in the night and camera flashes accompanied them. Raymond watched the news in the morning and the streets were still filled with bodies, living and dead.

He turned it off and went to the window and cracked it open. He leaned on the sill and looked out at the gentle flow of the river beneath the bridge and watched men and women pass, laughing, along the alleyway beneath his window. It was calm and peaceful here. He had been entirely undisturbed through the night.

Moonlight through the glass on curves of the white duvet draped across pale flesh. He'd slipped out of her room early when her breathing fell steady. It was the nature of his work.

He put a pan on the burner and let it warm. He filled the kettle with water from the tap. He turned it on and cracked two eggs into the pan. He watched them begin to solidify, whitening along the bottom of the pan, spreading quickly and unevenly. He used a spatula to try to give shape to the edges, then left them to cook.

The kettle boiled and he made a mug of coffee. He put two slices of bread in the toaster and then took the pan off the heat, shutting the burner off as he did.

When the toast popped, Ray buttered it and set the eggs on the slices with the spatula, then sat down to eat. The eggs were fresh—the yolks rich and yellow.

When he finished, he took the leftover crusts to the window. He carefully set them on the sill outside. He washed the plate and pan, then sat down beside the window again to finish his coffee. A pigeon dropped to the sill and ate the crusts. It stood looking in, then fluttered away to land on a metal gate below. He could hear someone rolling a trolly along the alleyway and closed the window. He refilled the mug and checked the time: ten o'clock.

Ray went into the bedroom and took a folder from his bag. He brought it out to the table and looked at it. He would need to destroy it, he thought. The boys might search the flat. If they found it, they would kill him. He opened it and looked through the pages inside. It was what the agency knew about the local players—almost nothing. Shortly after the Troubles began, the IRA split into two factions, the Provisional IRA and the, more Marxist, Official IRA. Provos were suspected of killing a high-ranking member of the Officials in a power struggle six months prior. The man was shot to death outside a house in Collooney in County Sligo. The most powerful member of the OIRA in the area now was Joe Costello in County Cavan, a labour activist involved in local politics. The Sligo Brigade fell under the Southern Command. The local leader was unknown. The cell might answer to a man named Sean Murray in Roscommon, a Sinn Féin figure from a hardline republican family.

Tommy Slowey had been in contact with a quartermaster in a neighboring county, Leitrim, before it fell through. He'd organized the arrival of shipments of guns on ocean liners from Boston. They were collected by fishing boats offshore, which landed somewhere on the Leitrim coast north of Sligo. Leitrim was harder to break into. It fell under the Northern Command. Ray sipped the coffee and flipped through the pages, familiarizing himself with what he could. Anything not committed to memory could be relearned. It was immersion that mattered.

He looked at the dossier for a while longer and then closed it. It gave him little more than a sense of things. He knew from experience that information in the dossiers was rarely entirely correct in any case. He took the coffee mug to the sink and set it down. He grabbed his jacket from the back of the chair, tucked the folder inside, and headed for the door. He locked it behind him and took the stairs down to the courtyard.

A young man leaned against the wall outside smoking a cigarette. He nodded to Raymond. The door behind him opened and a woman stepped out. He said something to her and she laughed. It was an inside joke, revelation of history. They joined arms and began to walk towards the stairs to the road. Ray followed close behind them. They took the stairs down to the street and pushed through the door. He stepped out after them with the folder clutched beneath his jacket.

It was quiet and empty on the street. The air was cool. He turned away from the town and began walking down the river. He walked until the pubs, shops, and flats came to an end and the road curved away from the river. He continued until he reached a forested area, trees along the shore. A narrow path, worn by use, led along the shore through the trees. When he was sheltered, he took the folder out and put his jacket on.

Ray sat down on the damp grass beside the water and took out his lighter. He set the folder down and opened it. He took half of the pages out of the dossier and held them up in the air by the corner. He flicked the lighter and held the flame along the bottom. The pages caught and began to burn. The flame rose and spread. Small black trails of smoke curled away. He felt the heat on his fingers. Ash flickered to the water, floating black on the surface.

When nothing but the corner remained, Ray dropped the paper into the water with the ashes. He could hear birds in the forest around him. Squirrels played in the trees, scuttling and twisting. He did the same for all of the pages, burning them and letting the ashes go. Then he burnt the folder, too, and watched the scattered black and white remnants sink and dissolve as they were carried in the soft flow of the river.

Ray put the lighter away and looked out across the water. On the other side, above the trees and buildings they hid, mountains rose against the white sky. They were short, round monstrous hills. They were green, black, or brown. Clouds were shifting around them. He watched the river and the reeds and the trees. He watched the swans on the other side, moving quietly. He had not seen them until now.

The swans drifted in the water, white necks curved. They stayed close, gliding effortlessly. They seemed to exert no energy. Small birds pulled from the trees and took flight. They rose and fell with fluttering bursts and landed gently on another limb. After a few moments, he stood and brushed off his pants and began to head back to town.

An old woman in a grey raincoat, dry, walking a small white dog, passed him at the entrance of the trail. She smiled, drawing the leash in. "Fine day."

"Isn't it just?" he replied. She continued past him and he walked up to the road, then followed it back along the river. He reached the town, walked up toward the bridge, and wandered through the center of town. He walked the streets absently, searching for logic, for patterns. He was forming a layout, internalizing it.

At noon, he met Slowey at the bookmakers. The bookmaker was a small shop on a corner on a dark side street up the hill. The streets around it were cold and narrow. Paint was fading. Windows and doors were boarded up or missing entirely. He stepped inside. Everyone glanced in his direction but no one looked directly. The gaze of people in the know.

The room was small. There was a counter at the back, where a man stood behind plexiglass. There were two small televisions mounted in corners near the ceiling. One was showing horse races, the other a fight. There were numbers on the wall and odds written on a chalkboard near the front. Two men sat on stools at a round table near the door looking at betting cards.

Slowey was leaning against the wall watching the horses. He turned toward Ray when he entered. "How's it going?"

"You got something down?"

"Promised City to place," Slowey said.

Ray leaned against the wall beside him and watched. "All set up for today?"

"Yeah. Two-thirty."

"See this shit in Belfast?"

"No. What?"

"Riots. Some kid was shot."

Slowey shrugged. "Nothing new there."

"I guess not," Ray said. "New to me."

"You'll get used to it." The low drone of the announcer and crowd carried from the speakers on the television. Horses began to cross the line, jockeys squatting low over their backs. "Pissah," Slowey hissed. He crumpled the betting slip in his hand. "That's gone. Let's get out of here."

Ray moved away from the wall and walked to the door without looking at anyone else. He pushed the door open. Slowey came out behind him. They walked down the grimy stones, smoothed and cracked with generations of wear. "You're going to have to tell me how this works before we go in there," Ray said.

Slowey cackled. "You'll know what you need to know. Guns come across and are unloaded onto fishing boats. The boats land and the guns are taken where they need to go."

"Who's on the boats?"

"Local men."

"What do you do then?"

"I coordinate," Slowey said, "Make sure it all goes according to plan."

"Bucky talks to you and you talk to the locals."

"That's right."

"So, we tell them how the operation runs and where to meet the boats. The rest is up to them. Is that it?"

"They're Bucky's men on the liners. I'll go along on the first ride. After that, it's out of our hands." He drew on his cigarette. "Now, you tell me. Where are you boys getting the guns?"

"They come directly from the base," Ray said.

"Then how can you promise there won't be a shortage?"

"There won't be," Ray said.

"You've got someone high up on the payroll."

Ray shrugged. "I'm just a soldier."

"Like hell," Slowey said. "Tell me you don't want to know how it works."

"All I care is that it does work."

"Have you eaten?" Slowey asked.

"Not since breakfast."

"Let's get something to eat," he said. "Never do business on an empty stomach."

They walked down to the chip shop and ordered food. They sat at the red counter along the edge and ate slowly. After that, they went across to the pub and ordered a drink.

When two o'clock came, Slowey looked nervous. "Listen," he said, looking over at Ray. "Gerry's a tough kid but I haven't met these other fellas. Some of the boys I've come across in this thing are as hard as they come, understand? Some could be the local postman but others are the butcher, feel me?"

"I've stood with real men, Tommy."

"And you think I haven't?" Slowey asked, sneering. "I'm a Southie, Ray. I ain't scared of nobody. But, I'm telling you, these men are serious."

"I hear you, Tommy. I'll watch your back."

"Watch your own back," Slowey said. "I've got mine."

At quarter after two, they walked down to Callaghan's. There was something ominous in the light in the windows, seeping out into the darkening afternoon. The clouds were thick overhead, filling the sky. Grey swells grew, shifted. They walked over the small bridge to the pub and Slowey opened the door.

Chapter 8

It was a small, long room with the bar at the far end, running along the left side. A hallway to the right led to the toilets. The rest of the room was a series of booths, tables, and stools. Everyone inside was in view at all times. Gerry sat with a sturdy looking man about ten years older than himself at a table in the middle of the room.

Another man stood behind the bar watching. He was slight and about seventy years old. His hair was white and thinning in the middle, revealing a round, shiny head. He wore a yellow button up shirt with short sleeves and had his arms folded over his chest.

Slowey led the way to the table. Neither man stood to greet them. "Tommy. How's things?" Gerry asked.

"Not so bad, yourself."

"Not a bother." Gerry tilted his head. "This is Liam."

"How're ya, lads?"

Ray nodded. "Raymond," he said.

"Have a seat."

Ray and Slowey each pulled out a chair and sat down across from the Irishmen.

"Will ye have a drink?" Gerry asked.

Ray noticed that neither man was drinking and shook his head. "No thanks."

Liam was examining him closely. "You're the new man," he said.

"I am," Ray said. "To these parts."

"And you're the man Gerry's been talking to," he said, looking to Slowey.

"Tommy Slowey," he said. "I had business with a friend of yours in Leitrim."

"So I hear." He leaned back and crossed his arms. "And that's the only reason you're in here today. But, sure, you know that yourself."

Slowey nodded again.

"Now, forgive me if I forgo the usual pleasantries, but I don't want to waste any time. Gerry tells me that you think you can do something for us."

"I do," Slowey said. "And it's the same thing I did for your friend in Leitrim."

"And the new man?" he asked.

"There's been some changes on the other side," Ray said. "The man I work for has taken over supply."

"Did that come with any trouble?"

"None. It's a matter of business."

Liam looked to Slowey, who nodded in agreement. "Gerry seems to be under the impression that you won't be expecting any payment for the shipments in question."

"That's not exactly true," Ray said, "only you won't be expected to come up with the payments yourself. A man on our end is taking care of that. Irish. Sympathetic."

"And who might that be?"

"It's a name you'd know," Ray said, "but, I don't think that I'm at liberty to say."

"So, you're in it for the money."

"We can't do anything if it's not profitable. That's just survival."

"And if the payments stop?"

"I'm American first. And Irish second."

Liam smiled. "See, that's the thing. To you, this is business. It comes down to dollars and cents. How can we trust that?"

"Everything's business."

"This isn't business to us," Gerry said.

"What is it, then?"

"This is our lives. It's about brothers and sisters abandoned in the North for the sake of peace down here. About betrayal by a pandering government and an occupation that goes back to time immemorial."

"We need to be able to trust you if we go into this together," Liam said. "What I don't want is one day to go out to sea and come back to shore with a boat full of guns to find the army waiting for us."

"Trust is easier when you don't start the relationship with a gun in your ear," Ray said.

"You have to know that we're serious, Ray. If you decide to go ahead with this, you can't play around. If we doubt you for a second, you'll get a .32 in the back of the head and you won't see it coming. This isn't America. There won't be any John Dillinger hanging off the car door with the Tommy Gun blaze of glory shite. There won't be any romance. It'll just be over. No funeral, even, because your body won't be found."

"And if it is," Gerry said, "it'll be half-buried in a field in Navan caked in cow shite."

"What are you saying?"

"I'm saying that this isn't like selling a pistol to Lucky Luciano for a stick up," Liam said. "You're supporting an armed conflict here, Ray."

"I understand that."

"Well, I hope you do," Liam said. "Until a few months ago we had a ceasefire going and we stuck to it. As it turns out, we should've been using the time to stockpile arms. The Brits will only ever play politics on their own terms. There's no winning on that front. That's been clear for hundreds of years, but someone somewhere forgot. So, I'll be blunt about this. We do need guns and we're going to be using them to wage war but we're only going to accept them if it's advantageous. If the risk is no greater than the reward."

"What put an end to the ceasefire?"

"Well, they blew up half of fucking Dublin, didn't they?" Gerry said.

"All of this is beside the point," Liam said, leaning in. "What we want to know is what are you proposing to do and how are you proposing to do it?"

Slowey leaned across the table, stopping only a few inches from Liam's face. "I won't pussyfoot around, Liam. I appreciate your discretion but I'm a man who likes to be direct." He took his pack of cigarettes out and offered them around, then lit one for himself. "We delivered five shipments to your friends in Leitrim, direct from Boston. Mostly guns from the war. MP40s, M1s, Brens, ammunition." He exhaled. "All without a hitch."

"It came to an end when O'Doherty was pinched and Meenan was killed," Liam said, "rest his soul." He was watching Slowey carefully.

"That's right," Slowey said.

"And you're proposing to do the same for us?"

"There'll be a few tweaks in the procedure, just in case your man let something slip under duress."

"I know Kevin," Gerry said, leaning back in the chair. "That's not a concern."

Slowey drew on the cigarette and peered at Gerry with pinched eyes. Ray could see him growing more comfortable already. "A pair of jumper cables in crafty hands can be quite persuasive. We'll be taking precautions."

"It's wise," Liam said.

"Now, here's the other thing," Slowey said. "With Ray here, we won't be dealing in antiques. This'll be Armalites, M16s, M60s, fuckin' sniper rifles. Top-grade."

Gerry looked at Liam, who leaned across the table with a new expression on his face. "How's that?"

"It'll all come directly from an army base," Ray said. "The crates will be loaded onto Tommy's boats in Boston and dropped off to your men here. After that, you do with them what you will."

"How are you getting guns out of the base?"

"The Vietnam War is over," Ray said. "We've got warehouses of guns with nowhere to go. Just sitting there, accounted for by men with no faith left in the government. Not just rifles and handguns, either. Submachine guns, Bazookas, surface-to-air missiles ..."

Gerry looked at Liam for a moment, then at Slowey, and then back at Ray. "Are you messing?"

Ray shook his head. "This is real."

"How much are we talking about?" Liam asked.

"There won't be any shortage," Ray said. "That's been seen to."

"How much?"

"It depends how long this war lasts," Ray said. "Two or three shipments a year. Maybe two-hundred-fifty guns a shipment. Fifty boxes of ammunition, a thousand rounds a piece. I don't know exact figures. The particulars will be hammered out."

"Jaysus," Liam said. He leaned on the table and put his hand to his mouth. The man behind the bar leaned on the counter looking on.

Slowey was grinning, yellow teeth peering out between his cracked lips. "It'll change the face of the war," he said. "The Brits won't know what happened."

Liam stared past the men. "And you don't want us to pay for these guns?"

"By the time they leave Boston, they'll already be paid for. All they want to know is that they'll be used. They don't want their money rotting in a hole in Wicklow."

"What the fuck do you know about Wicklow?" Gerry asked.

"How soon are we talking?" Liam said.

Ray glanced at Slowey. "We can have a small shipment, a test, arrive within two weeks. A few crates of guns and some ammunition. All we have to do is make the call."

"And you vouch for Tommy here, Gerry?"

"He brought in those shipments with Fergal and Meenan. You've seen the guns yourself, Liam."

"And you've no doubts about this man beside you, Tommy?"

"He's well connected in New York," Slowey said, running his hands through his slick hair. "I once seen Bucky cut a man's tongue out for giving his address to a delivery boy." He laughed. "He wouldn't work with anyone not vetted."

"Right so," Liam said, leaning back. "Now, I've got to talk to a man about some things. Gerry will be in touch."

Chapter 9

Aoife had green eyes. He didn't know exactly what it was about them but there was kindness in them, a curiosity and an openness that betrayed her. It was the eyes that confirmed what he already knew. That she was his way in.

She was standing along the bridge outside the pub when he left it, and he knew, then, that she had known he was inside, that she had some business or pleasure to attend to behind the doors but knew that she needed to wait to do so.

He could see those eyes across the way. She wore a beige mohair sweater and jeans and leaned against the wall. Her hair was dark. He took out his cigarettes and lit one, then turned to Slowey. "I'll catch you later," he said.

Slowey looked up at Aoife standing against the wall along the bridge and shook his head. "Don't go there, Ray. You want a piece of ass I'll take you to a place. There's plenty of fish in the sea."

"The heart wants what the heart wants, Tommy."

"Oh, Jesus. Do whatever the fuck you want. Just don't fuck this up for us."

Ray smiled and started walking slowly toward Aoife. She watched Slowey walk away and knew that he was coming for her. She waited at the bridge, watching casually. He stopped in front of her and stood there. "Hey," he said.

"Hey," she said. "You're the fella from the chipper."

"That's right," he said. "Will you have a drink with me?"

She looked past him to the pub.

"Somewhere other than here," he added.

She looked at him, searching. "I don't think that's a good idea."

"Just a drink."

The heron was back on the river, standing in the shallows near the edge of the bridge. The wind was blowing softly and it caught the tangles of her hair and drew them across her cheek. "Alright," she said, reaching up to brush the loose strands aside. "Let's have a drink."

"Know a quiet bar?"

"Yeah," she said. "I know a place." They walked together over the bridge and up a narrow street, tilted with a gently sloping incline. She walked slowly and steadily, taking every step with care. She was thinking. "So, you're the man from New York," she said, eventually.

"I am," Ray said. "You've heard of me."

"I have," she said. "A friend of Tommy Slowey's."

"I just met him, to be fair."

"So, you're not a friend?"

"I didn't say that," Ray said.

"I'd like it better if you weren't," Aoife said, looking up at him.

"And why's that?"

"He's a pig," she said.

"Ah, he's just a poor boy from South Boston turned into a hard man," Ray said. "I've met many worse."

"I'm sure you have."

They walked further up the incline and then turned up another narrow street to the right. There were shops and restaurants, and the light was full, though the sun was dropping lower in the sky. A man sat begging in a doorway bundled in blankets. People walked and talked and laughed.

"Why is it you want to have a drink with me?"

"Is it hard to believe?"

"No," she said, "but it's the reason I'm interested in."

"I don't know," Ray said. "How do you explain these things?"

"Carefully," she said. She pointed to a pub on the next corner. "There's a nice place here." The pub had large windows but the interior was hidden by wood panels and stained glass. They crossed over to it and she opened the door.

They sat at a booth in a corner near the back. The booth had a wooden table nestled against the wall. A dim brass lamp in the center, frilled with a yellow shade. The benches were tall with red velvet cushions and stained-glass inlays. Blue swirls, red arcs, purple streaks.

The wall beside him was stone and a mirror hung on it with a Jameson advertisement printed across it. The ceiling was paneled and white. On the other wall were framed ads, brass lamps, and an old wooden display shelf near the ceiling that held glasses and flowers in an old jug and whiskey bottles of age.

Aoife went to the bar and ordered drinks. She came back and sat down, looking at him again. "What's your name?" she asked.

He laughed. "Raymond," he said. "Raymond Daly."

"Aoife," she said. "Kelly."

"Nice to meet you, Aoife Kelly."

"Wait and see if you still think so in an hour."

A woman came over with two pints and set them on the table. "Now," she said, smiling.

"Thanks."

The radio was low and the hearty laughter of old men carried from some nook on the other side of the pub. "Sure, he was a well-known character around town," someone said.

"So, you're a cousin of Gerry's," he said.

She cocked her head. "How do you know that?"

"Slowey told me."

"I am," she said. "And you're doing business with him."

"I am."

"So, we'll be seeing a bit of one another I'm sure."

"I hope so," Ray said.

"He wouldn't like you taking me out," she said.

"Why not?"

"Because you're not one of us."

"One of who?"

"You're not from our world, our community."

"Maybe you're giving him less than his due," Ray said.

"I didn't say it was a bad thing." She lifted her glass and took a drink.

"Tell me," Ray said. "What does a girl like you do around a town like this?"

"Same thing a girl does anywhere, I reckon."

"And what's that?"

She shrugged. "A bit of this and a bit of that."

"You don't make conversation easy, do you?"

"I didn't ask you out," she said.

"I'm only teasing."

"I like the way you talk," she said. "You sound like James Caan."

He laughed. "That's funny, I was going to say the same thing."

Aoife laughed then too. "Is this your first time in Ireland?"

"It is."

"How do you like it?"

"My grandparents emigrated, so it's nice to see but I haven't seen much of the country. I came right from Dublin to Sligo."

"Have you been to the beach?"

"No," he said.

"You'll have to. There's not a whole lot else in Sligo. Where are your grandparents from?"

"Cork, I think."

The last rays of sunlight were falling to the table between them through the window, taking the colour of the stained glass with it. The knot on the glass was cast onto the table before them. As the sun dropped lower, it slowly spread, shifting across the pattern of wood grain.

Aoife was looking at him with something like curiosity in her eyes. It was a moment of reflection foreign to him, alien. He looked into her green eyes, searching for passage into whatever depths had taken her. He wondered if she sensed his deception— if she knew that he was lying to her. He was not sure of himself, yet. This was still new to him.

"What do people watch around here, soccer?"

"Soccer," she said, smiling. "Football, yeah they do. The English clubs."

"Really?"

"Yes," she said. "It's only Brits out 'til the telly comes on. There's GAA too, Gaelic and hurling. Depends where you are."

"Those are Irish?"

"They are."

"On TV too?"

"It is. It wouldn't be professional, now. They're local teams. Liam's brother Dermot plays for Sligo." She was watching him again. "You met Liam today, didn't you?"

"I did."

They continued to drink and talk, and the sun dropped lower still. It grew quiet and dark. "Do you listen to music?" he asked.

"Listen to music? Who doesn't?"

"I don't know," he said.

"I do," she said. "I'm kind of all over the place. Velvet Underground, The Jam, New York Dolls. Cock Sparrer."

"Cock Sparrer?"

"It's a band."

"Jesus Christ. I don't even want to ask."

"They're good."

"I'll take your word."

"What do you listen to?" she asked.

"David Allen Coe, Waylon Jennings, Willie Nelson, I don't know."

"God help us," she said.

"I like the Stones too."

"Right," she said.

"Do you listen to Irish music? The Chieftains? The Dubliners?"

Her lips twitched and she smiled. "You're a strange man, Raymond Daly."

He didn't know what she meant so he didn't dare fuel it. "I love the way you say that."

"What?"

"Raymond Daly."

"That's your name, isn't it?"

"It's something else in your mouth." He was looking at her lips, full and pink. To be it, he had to live it, to feel that it was true, so he was looking at them with longing. She was looking back at him, and he saw that she saw it in his eyes and felt a surge of fulfilment, of pride. It was the game. "What are you looking at?" he asked, because he knew when to shift the burden.

"I was going to ask you the same thing," she said.

"Great minds."

"Fools seldom differ."

He smiled. It was real. "Want to get out of here?"

"And go where?" she asked.

"Anywhere you want."

"Ok," she said. "Let's go."

He stood up and slipped his jacket on and they walked out of the pub together. He felt the eyes of the barman and the old man sitting at the barrel in the corner on them as they left. He didn't look back. He pushed the door open and held it for her and she stepped outside. The sun was dropping behind the roofs and the clouds in the sky were turning pink.

She began to walk down the road, moving slowly. He walked beside her, letting her lead the way. The buildings were worn around them. Some were shuttered and dark. "Did you grow up in Sligo?" he asked.

Aoife shook her head. "I was born in Fermanagh."

"Where's that?"

She walked along the curb, balancing, placing one foot in front of the other with care, like a child. "The North."

"When did you move down here?"

"When I was a girl," she said. "About eight or nine."

"With your family?"

"My mam."

"Why?"

She stopped walking and turned to look at him. There were no streetlights and the shadows fell across her. She stood between two cars parked along the edge of the street. "You've a lot of questions, haven't you?"

He laughed. "Sorry. I'm just interested, I guess."

"In what?"

"In you."

She tilted her head slightly. "Why?" It was a serious question. He saw the hint of suspicion in her eyes, though she did her best to hide it.

"What do you mean why?" he asked, laughing again.

"Why are you interested in me, in particular?"

"Should I not be?"

She smiled. "No," she said. "You shouldn't."

"And why's that?"

"Because I'm not some Manhattan girl," she said.

"A Manhattan girl?" he asked, laughing. "What does that mean?"

"I don't know," she said. "Class, elegance, socialites."

"You've never been to New York, have you?"

"No, I haven't. Is it that obvious?"

"I grew up above a Chinese restaurant across the street from a strip club," he said. He turned and started walking again, moving slowly still. She followed alongside, spinning on one foot to turn.

"Really?" she asked.

"Yeah."

"Your mother must have loved that."

He smiled. "Yeah, it was easy to run home between shifts."

She laughed, unsure if he was joking or not.

"But I'm not really from New York," he said. "Not the city. I'm from Buffalo."

"Where's that?"

"A little further north. Closer to the border."

"The border?"

"To Canada."

She kept pace with him, watching her feet as she walked. Her hands were in the pockets of her coat. "Really, though. Why are you interested in me?"

He looked over. "Is it so strange?"

She gave a half smile but didn't respond.

"I don't know. I guess I was just interested since you walked into that chip shop. Then I saw that you knew Gerry and … I don't know. I thought we might get along."

"We don't come from the same worlds," Aoife said. "If that's what you thought."

He shrugged. "Might be more similar than you think."

She shook her head. "There's nowhere else like this," she said, seriously. "You don't know what it's like. You might think you do, but you don't."

"I'm Irish too," he said.

"No you aren't," she said, laughing. "But it's not even that. Even Irish people don't know. People in Sligo don't know what it's like. Not really."

"What do you mean?"

"What goes on in my family, in my world, doesn't affect them. They go on about their lives without thinking twice about it," she said. "People from Sligo take holidays in the North, for fuck's sake—the absolute cheek." She laughed, and then turned serious again. "Unless you're in it, you don't know. Unless you come from where I come from, you can't know."

They reached the end of the street, and she led him around the corner. He followed her until they reached a gap. An old stone building sat in the shadows. The sky was dark overhead. The silhouette rose up, but he could make out none of the features beyond a tower stretching up from the middle. A stone wall and iron gate around the small stretch of land separated it from the public road.

"Have you been to the Abbey yet?" she asked.

"No."

"Come on. I'll show you." She led him down away from the road to the grass. She grabbed onto iron bars and pulled herself up to the top, climbing over. She dropped down on the other side silently. Ray glanced over his shoulder and then followed her over.

They walked across the soft grass, glistening with the hint of recent rain, until they reached the outer wall of the Abbey, a large stone building, like an old cathedral with no roof on top. It had tall, narrow archways running along the sides, nearly the entire height of the building. The walls were thick, strong.

"When was this built?" he asked.

"Twelve hundreds sometime," she said. She stepped through an archway into the middle of the stone. It was quiet and cold. There were carvings in the walls. Monks and crosses. Stories from years gone by.

"When did they stop using it?"

She shrugged. "They never did. When I was a teenager, we used to come here to get drunk. I'm sure they still do the same."

He laughed. She turned to face him. "Can I kiss you?" he asked.

She was looking into his eyes. "Well, aren't you the gentleman."

"Only at first."

"Yeah," she said. "I think you'd better kiss me."

"Better me than some sick bastard who listens to Cock Sparrer."

She kissed him. When they parted, they were standing in the middle of the cold stone. Moonlight came down through the arches around them. It was a place where there were centuries of history, of love and violence.

Blood had been spilled on the stone, seeped into the earth. Had been consumed, drawn upon, become part of the earth and the grass that had grown up after, inseparable. It was cyclical, repetitious, unending.

Chapter 10

The rhythm of raindrops on the glass was soothing in the early hours. He liked to crack the window and let the wet air into the flat. It seemed to rinse it—cleanse it.

The toast popped. He took the slices from the toaster and set them on the yellow plate beside it. He lifted the knife and buttered the toast, watching it melt. He poured his coffee and took a seat beside the half open window listening to the empty broadcast coming out of the radio in the corner.

Aoife was on track. He just needed to maintain the trajectory, to allow things to unfold. There was an undeniable pull to her. It was not a problem. He had to be immersed and authentic—to feel that it was real.

He sipped the coffee. A wave of warmth. It was the same principle as any entrapment. A matter of gaining trust. Of establishing dependence. Of exploitation. He had no illusions about that. To maintain illusions would mean ineffectiveness, weakness.

A pigeon dropped to the sill beside him, standing on the painted grey and looking through the glass. It shuffled. It glanced around nervously. It had no reaction to the rainfall. The rainfall was natural, inevitable. Unavoidable. He remembered a girl in college he'd misled, informed on. She was a communist, an activist. She had trusted him. She had been naïve and well-meaning. It was the well-intentioned who did the most harm.

Aoife was republican by nature. It was something bred into her. A worldview established at birth. He had no issue with republicanism. It was natural enough. It was a matter of self-definition, here. It was not pragmatic in contrast to British force. England was a democratic country, bar the monarchist pretensions. It could be reasoned with and understood.

He got up and dropped the crusts on the sill through the open window. The pigeon shuffled over and pecked at the bread, picking pieces with its beak. He sipped his coffee and watched through the glass, just inches from the bird.

After a moment, he turned and went back to the bedroom. He dressed and came back out. He shut off the radio and closed the window, then set the empty mug in the sink. He grabbed his jacket, slipped it on, and left the flat.

It was a mild day, and the air was soft, drizzle falling. A mist. He didn't get wet, just damp. He went down to the street from the courtyard and opened the door. He walked up the road. There was a small café not far down the block with a few chairs set up outside. There was no one at them for the rain.

He went up to the café. It had a glass front. He could see the customers and workers inside in the glow of artificial light. He opened the door and went in.

"Just a coffee," he said.

"Alright, then. And will that be everything?"

"It will."

"Grand. I'll bring it out to you."

He went to a corner near the window and sat down. He'd gone to university on a scholarship—ended up at Yale with the sons of men he hadn't heard about but was supposed to know.

The names held in awe back home were athletes, union leaders, and heavies.

Four years at Yale changed his perspective. He studied literature, of all things. History, too. He started at Yale in '68. The Vietnam War was in full swing. Support was faltering. He didn't get sent over and it was a matter of pride. Somehow, it seemed like resistance to reckless policy. He wasn't a grunt, humping through lice-infested jungles, crawling through collapsing muck tunnels.

Yale was a liberal school. Ivy League. There were communists on campus, but they were watched with care. Somewhere along the line, he was recruited by a professor—the head of American Studies. When he graduated, he had a job and a career. It was a path of service. A more precise, less savage, form of war.

The girl set his coffee down on the table in front of him. "Thanks," he said.

"Not a bother."

He picked up the cup and took a sip, watching people through the window. It was too hot, so he set it back down. "Billy Don't Be a Hero" played from the radio behind the counter. It was quiet and tinny. The rain started. A few drops fell, then petered out. He drank the rest of the coffee slowly and had another, then went back out to the street. There was an unease he couldn't shake.

From there, he wandered until he came across a small second-hand bookstore. A green hand painted sign over the door read Used and Rare. He opened the door and went inside. The store was small and tight. Shelves ran along both walls and up the middle. A small counter at the back had a cash register. An old woman sat behind the counter looking across at him, peering with difficulty through half-inch lenses.

At the front of the store, he saw an Irish Interest section. Books about the famine, the rising, the war of independence, civil war. There were guidebooks and travel books, recipe books and local histories. It was hot inside. The room was cluttered, and the old woman stared at him still, searching for a distinctive feature that would allow her to identify him. He smiled and went back over to the door and stepped out.

The air was welcome. He wandered further, absently. It was boring but he had to take his time. Matters like these couldn't be rushed. He walked until he came across a cinema on a side street with a sharp slant. The cinema lights were on. A horizontal sign descended from above the door that read Bohemian. Beside the red double door, there was a sign with showings listed. *The Man With the Golden Gun* in forty-five minutes or *Teenage Seductress* in an hour.

He looked at the poster for *Teenage Seductress* for a long time:
When She Was Good
She Was Very Good
When She Was Bad
She Was TORRID!

He glanced over his shoulder, embarrassed by how long he spent staring at the blonde girl unbuttoning her blouse, but there was no one around, so he looked a little longer. In the end, Roger Moore was more enticing with the PPK. He wasn't unaccompanied either and she didn't hurt the case.

Ray walked further up the road and looked through the window of a charity shop. It was small and cluttered with old clothes on hangers and trinkets filling shelves along the walls. He opened the door. The bell rang quietly above as he stepped through. Another small woman with thick glasses sat behind the counter. This time she had a brown turtleneck and a string of plastic pearls.

"Good morning," she said, looking up at him through the shields. Her orange hair was curled to a near afro around her head.

Ray walked past her, looking down at the coats hanging in the center of the store. He stopped and touched the sleeve of a blue shirt. He took his hand away. It felt grimy, powdery. At the back of the store he saw three shelves of books. They held mostly doorstop paperbacks, cookbooks, and discarded nonfiction with a small shelf of classics and literature near the bottom.

He looked over the fiction titles: *Evening in Byzantium; Jonathan Livingston Seagull; August is a Wicked Month; 84 Charing Cross Road; Once Is Not Enough; The Matlock Paper; The Day of the Jackal.* He picked up the last. Frederick Forsyth. He looked at the back cover, then opened the first page: *It is cold at six-forty in the morning of a March day in Paris, and seems even colder when a man is about to be executed by firing squad.*

That'll do it, he thought. He closed the book and checked the price, then brought it up to the counter. He checked his watch and paid, then went out onto the street again. He still had half an hour to kill. He walked back up to the cinema and opened the door.

It was dark and gloomy. The lights were low and artificial. There was no one inside except for a greasy kid behind the counter. Ray bought a ticket for James Bond and then went to a bench along the wall and sat down with the book.

He tried to read but he just kept returning to Laos. The dull slap and the tear, and the blood and brain on the amber wall. There were other memories too. There were rice fields and green mountains and men tied to chairs in cold rooms with little light. There were chopper blades and laughing men and happy children. There were women too. Women stooped with sacks in fields and smoking in doorways and dancing in sequined dresses.

There was the kid. Always the kid. The dull slap and brain matter. He knew that one day it would fade. It was that knowledge more than the knowledge that it was the right thing to do, that it was necessary, that allowed him to continue on. The kid was gone and one day his memory would be too.

He read for a while, then he went up to the counter and bought popcorn and a Coke. He crossed the room and went through the doors to Screen 1, where he took a seat in the middle. There was no one else there.

He sat alone in the middle of the room with the dark, false light surrounding him. Rows of empty seats on every side. The screen was still dark. He took a drink and waited. Two teenage boys came in and sat near the end of the aisle. A young couple entered next and sat somewhere near the back.

The room darkened, screen alight: a cylinder and gunshot; the spread of blood; sand and the grey lap of otherwise still water; a dark cliff overhang, crest out of view; dark clouds somehow tranquil; a woman, smooth and bronze; straight hair a solid form; subtle curves: eyelashes black and long, cheekbones swelling, eyebrows arcing, the purse of soft lips; oriental yearning, fear; a small man, a token, a gimmick; an envelope of money; a house of mirrors and nightmare; a belly dancer swaying, skirt glimmering; black lace; gold; guns; pleasure; conquest.

When he left the cinema, the afternoon was waning. He remembered a brothel over there—the sticky stench of opium between the walls, young bodies sticky with sweat. He walked back into the center of town, walked the streets and the river and watched the people around him, slow and constant. There was chatter and prolonged goodbyes. He noticed an uncertainty in Irish men, a lack of confidence, of self-assuredness.

After a little while, he saw Slowey coming out of a newsstand on the corner. He had a Coke in one hand and was looking down at change in the other. Ray crossed over. "Tommy," he said.

Slowey looked up. "How're things, Ray?"

"Not so bad."

"What are you up to?"

"Nothing. Just saw the Bond movie."

"Roger Moore, is it?"

"Yeah," Ray said.

"Ah, he ain't all that tough." Slowey cracked the seal on the Coke he was carrying. "I was hoping to run into you," he said. "I just got off the line with Bucky. The shipment's coming in the day after tomorrow."

"That soon?" Ray asked. He hadn't received word from the Company. He wondered if he should contact them himself. "Do the boys know?"

Slowey took a drink. "What are you doing tonight?" he asked.

"Nothing planned," Ray said. He was distracted. The Company had promised not to leave him naked, alone. Yet, it felt like he was in the dark.

"I'm going down to the Glenside with Gerry."

"I might take it easy."

"We'll be taking it easy," Slowey said. "It's a good spot. There's a pool table."

"Yeah."

"Come on down," Slowey said.

"Yeah, alright."

"Around eight."

"I'll stop by," Ray said. Slowey nodded and continued on.

Ray walked the streets and had another coffee, then went back up to his flat. He cooked a steak and potatoes and ate beside the window with the television on across the room. He washed the dishes and watched the bird on the ledge outside the window for a little while, and then went back out and made his way over to the Glenside.

Gerry and Slowey were at a pool table near the front of the bar when he walked in. Gerry leaned across, resting the cue on the bridge he was making with his left hand. He took a shot and watched the cue ball roll. It was straight and steady. He stayed low to the table until it hit the yellow he was aiming at. He straightened up and watched it roll to the corner pocket, gently brushing the cushion a moment before the fall.

Slowey grunted. Gerry lined up another shot. Ray walked across to them. "How's it going?" he asked.

Slowey watched intently as Gerry took an easy shot in the corner, drawing the cue ball back into position for a third along the side. "I'm being hustled," Slowey said. "Son of a bitch said he doesn't play and he's on the table like a skinny Minnesota Fats."

Ray watched Gerry shoot and wondered if he knew about him and Aoife. It was hard to tell. He looked at the half-empty beers on the little round table beside Slowey. "Finish those," he said. "I'll get the next. What are you drinking?"

"Smithwick's."

"Smithwick's?"

"Yeah."

"Alright." He went up to the bar and leaned across it. There was a girl behind it. "Three Smithwick's," he said.

"You're at the pool table?" she asked.

"Yeah."

"I'll bring those over to ye."

"Thanks," Ray said. He paid and went back to the table.

Gerry was still running. His hand was firm and the clicks were solid. The balls dropped into pockets definitively. Voices carried to them from a table nearby, muscling over one another: "That's your only one. Don't think you'll be going out tonight just because you've had a taste … I'm better off myself, you know … Ah, he was a great character around the town."

They drank and played pool. If Gerry knew about Aoife, he said nothing. He gave no indication that he did and Ray had the sense that he would not be shy. It was better this way, he thought. He could win Gerry over before he learned about Aoife. Ease him in. Establish his character. Play him the same way he was playing the woman.

"Where'd you grow up, Gerry?" he asked.

"Sligo," Gerry said. "But my mother came down the year I was born, so I'd be a bit of a Northerner at heart."

"Do you ever go back?" Ray asked.

"Once in a while," Gerry said. The speakers somewhere were playing low.

I remember
when we used to sit
In the government yard in Trenchtown

Ray lit a cigarette. Tobacco on his tongue like earth before smoke numbed the taste. He watched the girl behind the bar, hair was falling down across her forehead. He thought of Aoife and wondered again if Gerry knew.

No woman no cry
No woman no cry

"Hear about the shit in Derry?" Gerry asked.

Ray shook his head and glanced at Slowey. Slowey's eyes were on a woman at the table beside them. Her eyes were anywhere else.

"Another attack on a Catholic family. Three men came through the back gate and shot the father and son at the kitchen table. Brains scattered across the fuckin' scones."

"Who were they?"

"Who?"

"The gunmen."

Gerry shrugged. "UVF. UDA."

"Are they British? Like, soldiers?" Ray asked. The song ended and Led Zeppelin came on. "Trampled Under Foot."

"Or just bootlickers," Gerry said.

"But they are connected to the Brits?"

"They are," Gerry said. "The UVF was founded by an ex-commando. They say it was MI5 approached him for the job."

"Do you think that's true?"

"It's true that half the members are in the UDR."

"UDR?"

"Ulster Defence Regiment. British army. We've had men witness meetings between them and British intelligence firsthand. Course, some of them are just psychopaths."

"Like yourselves, then," Slowey said.

Gerry laughed. He seemed drunk and good-humored.

"You've known Liam a long time?" Ray asked.

"Long enough," Gerry said.

"And who's the old man?"

"The old man?"

"Behind the bar that day we came in."

Gerry set the beer down. "That's John Boyne. That's his bar."

"He's sympathetic?"

"You ask a lot of questions."

"I'm just wondering, I don't know. It's new to me."

"Wide-eyed and bushy-tailed."

"Forget it."

"He's on the town council for Sinn Féin," Gerry said. "You tell me something now. What do you do in New York?"

"What do I do?"

"Yeah. What do you do?"

Ray laughed. "I do this."

"You're a hood. A gangster."

Ray laughed again.

"Drive around in Cadillacs and Lincolns, is it?"

"Something like that."

"And you too, Slowey?"

"I drive a Malibu," Slowey said. "Or, I did. It's sitting in a garage collecting dust now."

They continued to drink. Ray had to work not to speak of Virginia suburbs rather than Buffalo streets. Their eyes were heavy and their tongues light. Stupor lifted them, elevating connection and interaction. They believed that they trusted one another. Guard fell. An openness emerged. Unnatural distance closed. They felt compelled to say what they felt. Compelled to lie too, to tell the story that came rather than one with grounding in reality, aware that there was truth in that too.

At a certain point, Ray found himself in the midst of a story designed to impress the men he sat with. He was drunk and that's when it was most dangerous to talk, but it was also when he had the most leeway and when the others were most likely to overlook inconsistencies.

"So, I was sitting at the table with a couple of street guys," Ray said. "And someone well connected."

"Mobbed up," Gerry said.

"Made."

"Jaysus." Gerry took a drink. The foam sat above his lip until he wiped it with the back of his hand.

They loved the hard stuff—the gangster stuff. It was the Hollywood effect. Ray glanced over his shoulder. "I shouldn't be saying this," he said.

"Who're we going to tell?" Gerry asked. "Al Capone?"

"No names," Slowey said, shaking his head. "No names." The words were slurred. His eyes remained on Ray. He, too, was eager.

"We were just drinking. No business. This guy had been … he'd been around a long time, you know? A guy we knew. A

84

neighborhood guy … lately, though, he'd been spending a lot of time with my buddy's ex and my buddy thought he was slipping it in … so they get to talking and things start heating up … flexing … then getting into arguing … you know? More direct, like."

"Yeah," Slowey said. "Yeah, yeah."

"Long story short, the wise guy told him … told him his cousin was …" he gestured with his hands, looking for words he could not find, "… well, and my guy took the bottle and stood up and cracked him across the dome."

"Fuck sakes."

"But the bottle had too much in it. Thick glass, you know? It didn't break."

"What happened?"

"His head split and he went down."

"Jaysus."

"And his legs started twitching but he didn't get up. We sat there looking at this and Johnny–"

"No names …"

"Buddy holding the bottle was staring down at the wop on the floor like he was looking at Hoffa."

"What did you do?"

"What could we do? If anyone found out, we'd be dressed in cement looking for oysters."

"Jesus Christ," Gerry said. "The fucking mafia."

Ray tilted the glass. "La Cosa Nostra."

"So, what happened?" Slowey asked.

"They never found him. He went away. Disappeared." He tilted his head slightly and looked across at Slowey. "That never gets back to Bucky."

Slowey brought his hand to his lips and turned it, lock and key. His eyes were fixed on Ray across the table.

"There's a man I knew," Gerry said, allowing the train of thought to continue to unfold, "I won't name any names. He made a mistake and repeated something he shouldn't have. Resulted in a good friend of mine in Derry getting arrested and turned over to the UDR. They tortured him to death."

There was silence. It was a war story of another kind. It didn't seem funny. "The man or your friend?" Ray asked after some time.

"My friend," Gerry said. "He died in custody. Couldn't have a proper funeral because his face was all disfigured."

"And what happened to the other man? The one who ran his mouth?"

"Like your Italian, he disappeared."

"It's getting late," Slowey said.

"It's half eleven," Gerry said.

Slowey looked at his watch. "So it is."

"We'll make tracks anyway," Gerry said. "There'll be good craic across at Boyne's."

They finished their pints and put their coats on, noisily scraping the chairs on the ground, trying to move with a steadiness that didn't betray their true state. When they stepped outside it was cool and quiet and light. They made their way along the curved street toward the river. The stone was wet beneath their feet. Cars passed at a distance, headlights broken by the slight mist in the air.

They walked up along the side of the river. Ray was breathing deep and taking in the world and it felt better than it normally did. There was a lift to it. His breaths were long and whole. They crossed the bridge and went up to the front of the pub. They could hear music through the door as they approached.

When they opened the doors, he felt the heat of bodies and the swell of sound came with it. A man with a guitar sat on a stool in the corner and the pub was in song.

Armoured cars and tanks and guns
Came to take away our sons
But every man will stand behind
The men behind the wire

Eyes turned to them. They found space at a table in the corner near the wall. Gerry disappeared for a while and Ray and Slowey tried not to look uncomfortable surrounded by republicans suddenly made uneasy by strangers. After a while, Gerry came back with three pints. He nodded to men as he passed and their attention fell away.

"Thanks," Ray said, taking the pint.

In the little streets of Belfast
In the dark of early morn
British soldiers came a running
Wrecking little homes with scorn

"That there's Kevin Foyle from Bundoran," Gerry said, gesturing to the guitar player. "Good lad."

Hear the sobs of crying children
Dragging fathers from the beds
Watch the scene as helpless mothers
Watched the blood fall from their heads

"It's a good song," Ray said.

Slowey laughed and lit a cigarette. He leaned in close enough for Ray to smell the unwashed hair on his head. "There's men here you wouldn't want to cross," he said. He was drunk. His words were clear but there was something missing in the context.

Ray nodded, wondering if something had been lost in the sound between them. "Yeah," he said. "For sure."

"I'm going to the gents," Gerry said. He stood up and disappeared into the mass, leaving Ray and Slowey alone at the table again. Ray felt the presence of the men around them and wondered if any were armed.

Armoured cars and tanks and guns
Came to take away our sons
But every man will stand behind
The men behind the wire

He slumped back in the seat and watched Slowey tap the ash from his cigarette.

Not for them a judge and jury
Nor indeed a trial at all
Being Irish means you're guilty
So we're guilty one and all.

Chapter 11

Along the main road, the earth was swollen, a slight frost to it. Black hills and mountains rose, blistering along the horizon. They drove through small and scattered clusters of buildings and then turned off the main road somewhere along the way.

They were driving out to the pier so they could take the boat out and meet the first shipment on the water. Ray felt a nervous energy inside. It was something that he first felt before a schoolyard fight as a child and something that he lived with now and embraced. This shipment would make or break the operation. He'd sent a coded letter the day before but received nothing in response.

The road was narrow. It was dark and the headlights only cast a faint glow ahead. They lit small stretches between the bends. Houses and barns emerged around bends behind walls and fences and yellow light shook from the windows. The van shook and trembled over ruts.

"Out that way there's a famine village," Liam said, gesturing off to one side of the road. "Deserted in those years. Nothing left but skeletons of stone and a stink to the earth."

Ray looked out but could see nothing over the curved field and stone wall. Nobody else spoke. They drove a labyrinth grid of winding roads. The country was small, Ray thought, but you could get lost out here forever. A few cars passed them by, slowing to a crawl and nearly scraping stone at the edge.

They drove a bend in the road along the coast, where the water was visible beneath the curve. "The Vikings landed on that island there," Liam said, pointing out to a dark shape in the water. "There was a monastery somewhere here."

"St. Patrick's Well is along the coast a little further," Gerry said. "Power of healing, so they say." Ray watched him in the narrow mirror above the dash. He didn't respond. He felt like a tourist. They slowed and turned toward the pier, where the trawler was waiting.

Aughris Pier was down a narrow, sloping strip off the road. The sea was out there, thrashing. They descended the slope. He thought about the history he'd read. Vikings landing, the island under siege. Sea swell and ships of conquest. The pull of desire. Of greed, exertion, and fantasy. The ecstasy of aggression, of unharnessed force. Visceral, fertile seizure—the grip of ripe, soft flesh.

The van slowed at the bottom of the slope. A fishing boat sat up out of the water on a frame beside them, dry and peeling. The pier was concrete and jutted out at a right angle from the sharp cliff. The cliff was dark rock. It was crowned with tufts of green earth, hanging over the edge like a fringe. The water rocked against the concrete wall.

A small blue and white fishing boat sat in the water, bobbing. Slowey coughed into his pale fist beside him and he looked across, reminded of his presence for the first time in a while. They rolled to a stop and Slowey got out of the van. Ray followed him, along with Gerry and Liam.

Dermot, Liam's brother, was standing on the deck of the trawler in the water. He wore a wool hat and a waxed coat. They left the vehicle at the pier and went down to the boat and boarded. They did not speak much as it moved away from the cement structure jutting out from the beach and the cliffside. The wake behind them grew silently, spreading a gentle ripple.

Shaking water on the deck of the boat. The shimmer of light reflected from the chain dangling beside the glass, fogged and dull, between the white and blue painted trim. The roof above caught the few droplets that fell from the sky—that rose from the water and met them. The motion, the roll of the boat in the waves, and the shadow of some dark steeple in the distance before the black and green shadow of the mountains against the grey sky.

The boat slid further from shore. Another craft lay out there, hidden from view by the night. Liam and Gerry stood along the railing, looking out. Dermot steered the craft, comfortable at the helm. The silence among them was not so much uneasiness as restlessness. Ray hoped that the shipment would be delivered without issue—that whoever was on board the other craft would do nothing stupid.

They moved out further into the sea, leaving the shore behind. Soon it was a low black strip. The lights of another boat at sea bobbed in the swell. They moved toward it. Slowey leaned on the side of the boat beside Ray, watching the lights shake through the fog. Ray drew his coat closer, burying his hands in the pockets.

The other boat grew. It soon became larger than their own. It remained dark as it neared though the rough texture that had taken hold across the bow over the course of life was visible in the moonlight passing between the clouds.

In the night, the silhouettes of men became visible on the deck of the other craft. The boat itself was rising and falling. It was a fishing boat capable of crossing the ocean. It carried thousands of gallons of fuel, thousands of gallons of bait. It could have been carrying tons of cargo. Tonight, it was likely carrying a smaller shipment. Just enough to make it worth the journey.

The boats drew close to one another. Dermot kept his eyes on the distance. The eyes of the other men were on one another, though the night meant that they could see only the shapes of faces. Lines were cast. The boats were drawn together.

There was a man on board, McIntyre. He crossed over to their trawler. He spoke with a South Boston accent. He stood with his hands in his pockets and cursed the cold. He spoke with Slowey and then shook hands with Liam and Gerry. He nodded to Ray, who stood back and smoked a cigarette. The discussion was brief.

After a few moments, crates were passed between the boats. They were set down on the deck. Liam lifted the lid on one with a crowbar and looked inside. He reached in and when he stood he was holding the black barrel of an Armalite. He held it in his hands and set it against his shoulder, looking down the sights.

He set it back into the crate carefully and a few more brief words were exchanged. The men shook hands again. McIntyre returned to his own craft. The lines were thrown back and the two crafts began to drift apart, decks rolling. Liam and Gerry were looking at the crates constantly.

They returned to shore and docked the boat. Gerry, Liam, Ray, and Slowey carried the crates to the back of the van and loaded them in. The body sagged with the weight. Gerry and Liam went back to help Dermot with the boat. Ray and Slowey got back into the van and waited. They were ashore and the guns were in the van. It was simple, clean.

When Gerry and Liam returned, they drove back the way they had come until they reached the main road again. It, too, was narrow and winding. They drove along and the headlights cast over bracken and bog.

Low stone walls rose and fell and broke apart. They passed farmhouses, barns, and the ruins of a castle in a field. They passed through hedges and forest and then through the flat grey walls of a small town. They drove through small streets until they reached a short warehouse near the far end of town. A man opened a metal gate, rounded pipe, and they drove into a dark parking lot.

The yellow beams sat across the pavement and curled up the very bottom of the warehouse before them. A metal loading door was hanging open. Ray couldn't see anything inside the building. He could just see the black bottom and the corrugated metal sheet dangling liminally.

A light came on inside the warehouse and he could see shapes in the dim orange glow. Gerry slowly rolled the van forward. The headlights washed across the building and into the open door. He rolled through, drawing to a halt just inside.

Two Ford hatchbacks were parked inside the warehouse. There were two people in the bay. The light was low and they were hard to make out.

Gerry shut off the van and opened the door. When Liam followed, Ray opened the back door and stepped out into the warehouse. The air smelled like dust and manure. It was then that he recognized the other people standing in the warehouse. John and Aoife. It caught him off guard.

Aoife was in the warehouse. It sank in quickly. They exchanged a short glance. She looked away first, so he went around to the back of the van, where Slowey was already standing.

"Aoife's a volunteer?" he asked.

Slowey shrugged.

"You wouldn't know it."

"Open the door," Liam said, coming around the back of the van. "Let's get these boxes unloaded."

The guns were taken from their crates and loaded into plastic bags. Magazines, barrels, and rounds. They worked in silence. The guns were bundled and thrown into the waiting cars. When they were done, Liam took one of the cars and was gone and then John took the other.

Gerry, Slowey, Aoife, and Ray stood in the warehouse. It was quiet. There was a man at the gate who Ray didn't know and who didn't introduce himself.

"You want a lift?" Aoife asked, looking at Ray.

Ray was surprised by the casualness of the phrase—as if they were leaving a party not smuggling guns.

"I'll run him home," Gerry said.

"What about Kevin?" Aoife asked, looking out into the lot, searching for the man standing somewhere in the shadow of the gate.

"You can take him," Gerry said.

"Fuck that," Aoife said. "So, he can try and put his hand up my shirt again?"

"Are ye never going to get over that?"

"Let's go," Aoife said. She walked beneath the door and out of the bay. Ray glanced at Gerry and Slowey, then shrugged and followed her out.

"You're a volunteer?" he asked.

Aoife smiled.

"You didn't tell me."

"Should I have?"

"It seems important."

"It is," Aoife agreed. She said nothing else. Ray followed her around the side of the warehouse. Aoife unlocked the door and they climbed into her pale yellow car. She started the car and they drove to the gate, where the faceless man let them out.

The headlights wove through winding roads, passages of sycamore, through the countryside. They drove slowly with the windows down. The stretch of bog and heather; deep blues of distant mountains against the evening sky; the smell of a turf fire hung in the air with the hint of smoke from a hidden cottage.

Guns had allure, an aphrodisiac quality. The absolute power they brought. It was not animal. It was something else, something greater. The memory of cold steel and the solid sound of magazine cartridges slotting into place stayed with them. Cartons of rounds, smooth and heavy and lethal.

They parked the car up above the beach. Headlights swept down across the sand to tumultuous ridges calmly rushing the shore. The moon threw light against the cloud. They could hear the thrust of waves rising and swelling, convulsing and crashing on the rocks; white froth spreading and flowing on the surface, stretching over stone, dissipating only to rise again.

The crash on the rocks was a gentle caress, softening, smoothing. There was no violence in it, only vigor—passion.

They got out and went down to the beach. It was cold and the sea breeze carried through their clothes. They took their shoes off and walked barefoot through the sand, feeling the grains against their toes, until they reached the rocks along the shore. The water lapped their bare ankles, biting the skin, and they stared out across the waves.

They did not hold hands but only because they did not need to. There was no distance between them. After, they went back up to the top of the beach and sat in the dry sand where it was deep and soft. The grains ran between their fingers and toes. The sand gathered in the knots on their sweaters. The wind was cool and calm and easy.

Chapter 12

"Do you want to go to a gig?"

"A gig?"

"Yeah," Aoife said, turning her head to look at him from the hood of the car. She lay on it with her hair splayed across the metal. The sound of waves on the beach below played through the wind.

"What sort of a gig?"

"At a farm not too far away."

"Like a concert?"

Aoife smiled. "Yeah."

"You do those out in farms here? Like in a barn?"

"Isn't that what your country singers do?" She sat up, resting her hands on the hood. "It's just a bunch of lads got together and organized it. A few bands. It'll be good craic."

Ray nodded. "Yeah, alright," he said. "Sounds like a good time."

"Fella I used to go with is in one of the bands." She grinned at him, as if she was joking, then hopped down off the hood of the car and went around to the door.

Ray walked around the car and opened the passenger side door. He climbed inside and shut it. Aoife turned the key in the ignition and started the car. The headlights played across the grass before the sand. As she backed up, the beams widened and then faded. She turned the car around and pulled back out onto the narrow road.

The car rolled over loose rocks and gravel with a crackling grind. Aoife glanced across at him, then reached down and turned on the stereo. A familiar song rose from the speakers around them.

Now, John T. Floores was a-working for the Ku Klux Klan
At six foot five, John T. was a hell of a man

He looked at the tape deck and then at Aoife. "Shotgun Willie," he said, grinning. "I thought you didn't like country."

"I decided to give it a go."

"And?"

"Some of it's not so bad," she said. "Ballads of working men, gunslingers, and heartache. It's like sitting in the pub on a Thursday night."

Ray sat back in the seat with his head lying against the headrest, watching her drive. The moon hung over the sea and the water caught the glow, spreading. He remembered driving through the countryside in a doorless jeep with the radio playing in another place. "American Pie" and "Heart of Gold." He remembered massive banyan trees, roots tangled and woven, limbs crossed and severed and overlapping. The sky clear and the world near empty, jeep rocking in the ruts and muck splashing up the matte green.

He was drumming his fingers on the inside of the door. He reached down and started to roll the window down to let the air through. "Keep that window closed," Aoife said. "Unless you want the absolute smell of shite coming off those fields." She paused. "Ah, fuck's sakes you've already done it."

Ray rolled the window back up, closing the crack along the top. The smell of manure had, indeed, seeped into the car. It was strong and pungent and earthy. It reminded him of the smell of foreign soil in Laos after the rainfall. It was not the same, yet it was distinct and earthy and seemed to embody something … he let his thoughts subside before Ireland and the absolute smell of shite fused together permanently in his mind.

As he watched Aoife guide the car, a twinge of guilt began to grow. He pushed that, too, from his mind. He had to remind himself of the bigger picture, of the insignificance of his deception in the grand scheme. He reminded himself that Aoife was a volunteer—that she had aided in bombings, in kidnappings. She was not innocent. She was not a victim but an active party in war, a combatant. He was a predator–it was his role.

He remembered that night in Laos when the boy was pressed against the wall looking down the barrel of the gun and the sweat was slick on his skin and he could smell the stale odour of his own oily hair, and the other men were looking at him looking for some kind of direction. He remembered making a decision then and the ripple of consequence, or inconsequence, that followed.

They wove through winding roads. Aoife turned onto a long laneway and began to drive up a sloping hill towards a farmhouse at the top. Cars were parked along the laneway near the top. The house was well-lit, and the barn a short distance from it was glowing. As they drove up the lane, drawing closer to the top, the muffled sound of a band playing carried across the field between them and the barn.

Weather stripped; the barn looked sunken in the ground. Aoife pulled the car to the side of the lane between two others. She shut off the engine and opened her door. Ray stepped out too and shut the door after him. They walked across the gravel to the soft grass.

They crossed the grass to the barn and went through the open side door, passing a small cluster of men and women lingering in the opening. They seemed to recognize Aoife but did not say hello. Ray felt their eyes on him as he passed. He felt out of place.

Ray made eye contact with a pale, greasy-looking man with long black hair parted down the middle. His eyes were cold blue and seemed nearly vacant. His cheekbones were sharp. Ray lifted his chin slightly, nodding. The man's expression did not change.

They entered the barn. The crowd was large and loud. There was a band on the far side of the room playing poorly tuned instruments on bad amplifiers. The words in the song couldn't even be heard, only the rise and fall of the drowning voice. Aoife began to move her body beside him, not quite dancing but there was rhythm to it. He felt the heat of other bodies in the room, the air thick with it.

"Hey, Aoife."

Ray turned at the sound of the voice. The man from the doorway was standing beside him, looking at Aoife. Aoife turned as well, looking at the man. Her expression shifted immediately. It was not pleasant. "Michael," she said.

"You're looking fit," he said. Aoife did not reply. She glanced at Ray. Ray kept his eyes on the man, the music grinding behind him. "How's Gerry?" he asked.

"What do you want, Michael?"

Michael stepped closer. He moved like he was drunk. There were two men standing just behind him. They moved closer with him but stayed silent. "I can't quite hear you," he said. "Let's go talk outside." He looked to Ray. "You'll excuse us, won't you?"

"We can step outside," Ray said, "but I'll be coming with you."

Michael's eyes narrowed. "Who are you? The American cousin?"

"Who the fuck are you?"

"Ray," Aoife said, reaching out to touch his arm.

"Thinks he's hard, lads."

"Thinks he's a real Al Capone," one of the men behind him said.

"The fuck is it with you Irish and Al Capone?" Ray asked.

"Piss off."

Ray looked back and forth between the men but did not reply. Without warning, Michael stepped forward and threw a right hand. Ray saw each movement. He saw the foot lift and the weight shift forward. He saw the twist in his hips and the hand begin to rise.

As soon as the hand moved, Ray stepped forward and threw a hard right hand of his own from the shoulder. It was a practiced motion and a straight punch—it closed the distance quickly.

Ray felt his fist connect with Michael's chin and the jaw give way beneath the force. The punch carried through, and Ray pulled his fist back to his chin quickly to protect himself. Michael buckled before him and collapsed at his feet, caking his white flesh in wet muck.

As soon as his body hit the ground, there was a surge. The two other men rushed Ray. As Ray watched the rush, he realized that the closest was now holding a small black knife.

Ray stepped back and then threw his weight into a leg kick. He aimed low and swung his foot through to the left, connecting with his target just below the knee. The knifeman's leg gave way and he stumbled to the ground beside Michael, who was beginning to rise, dazed by the blow he'd received to the jaw.

The second man closed in and grabbed onto Ray from the left hand side. His hands clamped onto Ray's shirt as he attempted to drag him to the ground. The fabric was pulled tight against his flesh, cutting into the skin around his neck. Ray could tell that the man was not an experienced fighter.

He drove his elbow into the man's ribs hard and then twisted toward him. He drove his elbow up into the right arm, clamped around his collar, and severed the grasp. Ray then pushed hard and sent the attacker stumbling back. He turned his attention quickly to the knifeman scrambling to his feet beside him.

His foot seemed to collide with the side of the man's face of its own accord—it was mechanical, automatic. It was the need to neutralize the threat by any means necessary. The man's head twisted and his torso sagged. Muscle memory and self-preservation took over. Ray stepped in and stomped hard on the falling head. His boot connected with the skull behind the ear and drove it down into the soft ground.

Aoife screamed. He felt her hands on his shoulders and stepped back, allowing her to guide him. The knife was lying in the mud beside the crumpled body. His back was rising and falling, still breathing. Michael was stooped beside his friend, looking at Ray, still stunned by the punch. The music was still roaring in the background.

Ray moved back further. "Let's go," Aoife said. The rest of the crowd around them had backed away or was beginning to close in. Ray nodded and backed away from the men himself, keeping Aoife behind his outstretched arm. None of the men moved toward them. He turned and pushed her gently. "Hurry," he said. "Let's get out of here."

They walked fast to the doorway and through it into the open air, then headed for the car. As they moved, Ray waited for the sound of a gunshot behind them. His back felt exposed, vulnerable. It was bare and without protection. But, the gunshot did not come and they reached the car. Aoife frantically opened the door, still unlocked, and forced the key into the ignition.

Ray grabbed the doorhandle and pulled the door open. He climbed into the car as the engine came alive. He pulled the door closed. Aoife turned the car around. The wheels spun, spraying gravel and dirt. The shrapnel peppered the other cars in the lane, ricocheting off doors and windows.

"Who were those guys?" Ray asked, as Aoife pulled out onto the road below the farm. The tires squealed as they turned.

"Stickies," Aoife said.

"What the hell was all of that about?"

"Nothing," Aoife said.

"Nothing?" Ray looked across. "You aren't about to tell me I just bludgeoned that poor lad for no reason." He paused. "That's it for him. He's not going to wake up tomorrow morning and shake that off."

"They're Official IRA," Aoife said. "They've got it out for Gerry."

"Why?"

"For something stupid."

"Something stupid he did or something stupid they did?" Ray asked.

Aoife didn't respond. Her hands were tight around the steering wheel and the car was running out onto the main road now, yellow beams winding across stone walls and tangled shrubs.

Ray watched the rear-view but nothing emerged—no shaking headlights and no silhouettes of dark vans. He waited for the sound of sniper fire, for the tear of a machine gun from one of the abandoned stone cottages in the dark slopes around them, but nothing came, and before long they were gone and he was laying back in the seat watching the narrow road and the sudden bends as the headlights cast forward.

Chapter 13

The window was open and the air was cold coming through it. The pigeon stood on the sill outside, looking through the glass. It shuffled up and down the length and stopped again. It tapped its beak on the glass and waited, looking in.

Ray pulled the crust off his toast and stood up from the kitchen table. He crossed to the window and stood in front of it, looking at the grey and white bird on the other side of the glass. The pigeon leaned in again and rapped on the glass with its small beak.

He reached up and held the crust through the gap, then dropped it onto the sill. The pigeon shuffled over to it and began to peck at the bread. He watched it for a moment, examining the strange thrust of the bird's neck, then turned away from the window and sat back down at the table.

The radio played quietly in the corner–the news. They were discussing some scandal related to government and building. He wasn't paying attention to the words. He watched the pigeon tap at the bread for a while longer, pulling pieces from his own toast as he did. He sipped the coffee and thought about Aoife and the men he'd fought the night before.

They were Official IRA, she'd said. Michael, one of them had been called. He tried to visualize him–pale and greasy looking. He'd recognize him if he saw him again. He wondered how bad the damage had been. He'd felt something break. Aoife was falling for him, he knew. He heard the floorboards creak and turned to look over his shoulder.

Aoife was standing in the hall in a long blue button up shirt with her red-brown hair falling over her shoulders and across the white skin over her collarbones. Her legs were bare and long beneath the shirt. She had her glasses on. He smiled at her, and she walked the length of the hallway, stepping into the kitchen.

"Want coffee?" he asked. Aoife nodded and sat down at the table. Ray stood and took another cup from the counter. He filled it and set it down on the table in front of her. "Milk?"

Aoife shook her head. "Black."

"Toast or anything?"

"No thanks."

He sat down at the table across from her and touched the coffee cup, shifting it absently. "What was that last night?" he asked.

"Can we not talk about it?"

"I might've killed that guy. I kicked him in the fuckin' head."

Aoife looked down at the mug.

"Who was he?"

"Michael," she said. "He used to … you know, hang around with Gerry."

"He was a volunteer?"

"Still is, I guess," Aoife said. "There was a disagreement and he went off and joined up with some of the others."

Ray looked at her closely. "What kind of disagreement?"

"Michael thought that the movement was starting to lean toward the right."

"It wasn't socialist enough," Ray said.

"Something like that," Aoife said. "But he always had a problem with Gerry. They never really got along."

"You said something stupid happened."

"Yeah," Aoife said.

"What was that?"

Aoife shook her head. "I can't tell you that."

Ray looked back at the window. The pigeon and the crust was gone. The sky was blue and a few white clouds hung above the rooftops across the alleyway. "Do you want to get breakfast?" he asked.

Aoife smiled. "No," she said. "That wouldn't do, would it?"

"What?"

"To be seen together like that."

Ray nodded. "Right."

"You're not going to get soft on me, are you?"

Ray shook his head. "All this sneaking around," he said. "It's hard to remember sometimes."

"I thought you'd be used to it," she said. "You know, being a gangster and all."

Ray smiled.

"You can handle yourself," Aoife said. "I'll give you that." She stood up and came around the table and touched the side of his face with the back of her hand. "I'd better get dressed." She walked past him and left the kitchen, then disappeared down the hall into the bedroom.

Ray got up and cleared the table. He set the cups in the sink and rinsed the crumbs from his plate. He washed out the cups and then set them to the side to dry. He listened to the quiet sound of her footsteps creaking on the floor as Aoife came back down the hallway and then stepped into the kitchen. He turned and looked over his shoulder at her.

"Right so," she said.

Ray nodded. "You're off?" he asked. It felt awkward. He turned to face her.

Aoife nodded back. "Yeah," she said. "I'm off." She lingered in the doorway of the kitchen for a moment and then turned away, stepping back into the hall. She disappeared from sight and then he heard the sound of the door opening and closing. He felt the reverberations in the wall and floor. Then her feet were on the stairs outside and eventually she was gone.

Ray tossed the cloth that he was holding on the countertop and turned up the radio. He listened absently to the sounds. They didn't register. He walked to the window and looked out over the sill to the alleyway below, wondering if Aoife would walk that way. He did not see her and wondered if she was walking too close to the building. He craned his neck and still saw nothing, so he turned away and rested his hands on the back of the chair he'd been sitting in.

It was growing complicated. She was growing on him in a way that he had not anticipated. He did not want to admit it to himself because it was an indication of weakness—the inability to remain detached. He knew, also, that he needed to break past this division she was creating between him and the rest of her life. She was keeping him isolated—it was intentional. In order for her to be worth anything to him, he needed to close the gap.

Ray left the kitchen and went into the bedroom. He picked up the Forsyth novel and then went back out to the hallway to put on his shoes. He took his leather coat from the hook and slipped his arms into its sleeves. He slipped the book into the jacket pocket and then he opened the door and left the flat.

He closed the door behind him and locked it, then went down the stairs to the rooftop courtyard. His shoes echoed off the hard steps. It was cold and grey outside and the clouds were threatening rain. He could feel the slight wetness in the air as he crossed the courtyard to the second set of stairs and went down to the street.

He stepped out into the street and let the door close behind him again. He walked up along the river to the newsstand at the corner. He went in and bought the tabloid paper, paying with change at the counter. He stepped back outside and walked up the street to a bench beside a garbage bin. He opened the paper and scanned it for an emergency code.

He saw nothing emerging from the articles. He skimmed articles about Mr. Heath and Mr. Benn. A headline halfway down a page spoke about Europe and the referendum. He read about Dana, Elton John, and Ann-Margret. When he was sure there was nothing in the paper meant for his eyes, he folded it in half and left it on the bench.

He wandered Sligo absently and remembered the last deployment. He remembered landing in a site where the Special Forces had tracked a man they were looking for. They burnt the hamlet and the smoke was like fog. It seemed to slowly fill the space around them and the scent of burning straw was thick, like the wails of the women and children.

The rest of the morning was spent walking and thinking. He went into a men's clothing store and looked at the jackets and shoes but bought nothing. He got another coffee and ate a sandwich. He found himself bored and alone in Sligo. He knew only the people he played. The rain held off. In the early afternoon, he walked along the street until he reached O'Neil's pub. He opened the door and stepped inside.

Tommy Slowey was sitting at the bar with a cigarette between his fingers and a pint of Guinness in his hand. His blue linen shirt draped loosely over his bony shoulders. His eyes flicked to the mirror when the door opened. He watched as Ray walked across the floor to the bar. There were three other men inside, and the man behind the bar.

"Ray," Slowey said when he sat down beside him. He didn't glance his way.

"Tommy," Ray said. He nodded at the barman. "A pint."

Slowey looked over at Ray. "Haven't seen you around in a while."

"I was in here two days ago." He lay a few coins on the bar and counted them out, then scooped up the extras and pocketed them. Slowey didn't answer. Ray watched the other people in the bar. The barman set his pint down in front of him and he picked it up and took a drink.

"Going to the races soon," Slowey said.

"I'll come with you."

Slowey nodded. He took a drag on his cigarette and then a sip of his beer. They sat silently together. After a while, Slowey finished his beer and looked at his watch. "Come on," he said, pushing out his stool. Ray finished his own and then got down off the stool and followed Slowey out of the bar.

They walked to Slowey's car and then drove to the track. Slowey put money on a horse called Loser Takes All and Ray followed suit. They sat down near the track and smoked cigarettes until they noticed Aoife and Gerry sitting a little further down.

Slowey caught Gerry's eye and nodded to him, and he waved them down. When they reached Gerry and Aoife, Aoife avoided Ray's eyes. She looked down at the ground and out at the track. Slowey and Ray greeted Gerry and sat down beside him. "Hey Aoife," Ray said.

Aoife looked across but didn't respond. "What's the matter?" Gerry said, looking across at his cousin. "Say hello."

"Hi," she said. She spoke quickly and looked away again.

Gerry looked at her and then at Ray. "What? Something happen between you two?"

Ray felt Slowey's eyes on him but didn't glance his way. He looked at Aoife. She shook her head slightly but did not speak. Gerry was still watching him. "Yeah," Ray said. "I guess so."

Aoife's face dropped. Her eyes were ice. Gerry stared through Ray for a moment and then looked at Slowey. "Jesus," he said. "I don't even want to know." There was a moment of silence and then he changed the subject. "Liam's around here somewhere too."

Ray and Aoife sat awkwardly on either side of Gerry. Slowey leaned back on the stands and put his feet up. Ray could see the shit-eating grin spreading across his face from the corner of his eye. They watched the race and, slowly, the awkwardness dissipated between them. If Gerry took offence, he did not show it.

Liam joined them soon. They went from the track to the same Chinese restaurant that Ray had been to with Slowey and they all ate together. From there, Aoife went home and the rest went to the pub. They drank and spoke of business and pleasure and the distance that existed between them gradually closed. The topic of women was not broached. As he drank, Ray thought about a woman he knew, Jolene. She didn't love him and never would and that was why he called her when he was feeling alone. Jolene was a woman and that was all there was to her. Aoife was something else.

They drank until it was late and then Slowey and Ray said goodnight to the others and left the bar that they'd found themselves in. They walked and the evening air was brisk. There was a slight dampness to the air, as there always seemed to be in Sligo. Ray heard that things were different on the east—that there were places where the sun shone often, but he didn't believe that entirely.

"Do you want to come by and have another?" Slowey asked, as they turned onto Wine Street and began down toward the center of town. It was the first time that Slowey had invited Ray into his home and, though he did not want to, he knew that he could not refuse the offer. It was early enough, in any case.

"Yeah," he said. "Let's have another."

It went on like that for some time. They drank and talked and went to the races. He spent time with Aoife, and they stopped shielding it so much from the others. He learned about her, and she believed that she was learning about him as well. Trust grew among them all.

In Sligo, time moved slowly. There was little to do. They went to the beaches and sat in pubs and ate fish and chips and Chinese. He constantly checked the tabloid for codes but nothing ever came. Guns continued to arrive on boats, and he stopped going along on the rides. Slowey did too.

Chapter 14

Liam pushed the door open and stepped out into the grey glare of the day. The fresh air came through the door and flooded Raymond. He followed Liam out of the pub with Gerry in tow. They moved with the slow gait of men with drink on them.

John Boyne was standing on a milk crate just outside the doorway changing a lightbulb. He looked down at the men as they stepped out. "Liam, how're ya?"

"Not a bother, John."

"And how's your mother?"

"She's well."

"Tell her I was asking."

"I will, John. Come by the house some afternoon," Liam said. "Sure, she'd love to see you."

John went back to the lightbulb. There was a chill in the air. Raymond put his hands in the pockets of his coat and stood beside Liam. Gerry started toward the parking lot to the left of the pub. There were half a dozen cars in the lot and a small van. The two other men followed Gerry toward the lot.

A grey Saab 99 was parked near the edge of the lot, just a few meters from the entrance to the pub. The lights came on. Raymond looked at the car. In the passenger seat, a man in a black balaclava was staring at Liam. The driver was out of view as the car was parked parallel. Another man in a balaclava sat in the backseat. The backdoor opened and a foot emerged.

"Get back!" Raymond yelled, he grabbed Liam by the collar and pulled him hard. Gerry turned sharply, following Raymond's eyes to the car. The passenger door was open and both men were stepping out of the car. Raymond turned and ran for the door of the pub. There was a resounding crack, then a rattle of gunfire. Shots echoed across the lot. Rounds ricocheted off asphalt and stone.

"Get down!" Raymond yelled to John, who stood on the milk crate with wide eyes. A bullet caught the wooden door beside him and embedded itself, sending splinters across his face. He twisted around, looking back at the car, and realized that the gunshots had stopped. The car doors slammed and the engine revved. Tires squealed as it pulled away from the curb.

Gerry was crouched, paralyzed, watching the car disappear. Liam was sitting on the ground clutching his stomach. His face was white. Raymond looked down to check himself for bullet wounds, then ran from the doorway to Liam. "He's been hit!" he called to Gerry.

Gerry turned to Liam. He looked in shock. Raymond put his hand on Liam's shoulder, crouching beside him. "Where are you hit?" he asked.

"In the belly," Liam said. He opened his hands and blood began to pool through his white shirt.

"Keep the pressure on that," Ray said. "We're going to get you help."

Gerry stood over Liam, looking down. "Jesus Christ," he said.

"We need to get him to a doctor."

John was down off the milk crate and suddenly had Gerry by the collar, shaking him. "Get the car," he said. He pushed him hard in the direction of the lot and stooped down beside Liam. "You alright, Liam?"

"I've been hit, John."

"You'll be alright," John said. "Gerry's getting the car. We're going to get you to Gabriel McGahern's. Gabriel will have it sorted."

"Who's Gabriel?" Ray asked.

"He's a doctor," John said. "A good man. One of us."

"Help me get him to his feet," Ray said. "Liam, can you stand?"

"I can," he said. He slowly rose. Ray and John supported him. Gerry pulled up along the edge of the lot in a blue Cortina wagon. He got out and opened the back door.

"To the car," John said. "Before the guards arrive." They hurried Liam to the car and helped him into the backseat as smoothly as they could. Liam grimaced but stayed silent. Blood began to seep onto the seats. Gerry climbed into the front and slammed the door. Ray closed the back door. "Go with him and I'll ring Gabriel here. I'd best stay to talk to the guards. I was inside and saw nothing."

Ray went around the car and got into the passenger side. Gerry shifted and spun the car around, tearing toward the street. He turned right as the sound of sirens began to grow from the other direction. The sky was blackening overhead. Rain was threatening to fall—he could feel it through the open window. When Gerry turned, Ray could feel the motion in his stomach. He did not envy Liam, groaning in the backseat.

Gerry could drive. Low walls and a series of identical looking houses passed them by, low to the ground. The sirens never drew nearer and the car slowed on the road in front of a small house just like all the others on the road. They were on a slight incline and Ray wondered if Liam could feel the weight of gravity pulling the bullet deeper.

He opened the door and went around to the side. The front door of the house opened and a large man with a wobbling belly in a tight T-shirt came out, hurrying across the lawn to the road. He opened the gate and passed between the low walls, approaching the car. "Help me bring him into the house," he said to Ray. His voice was deep and cool, reassuring. "Park around the corner," he added, looking to Gerry.

The doctor helped Liam out of the car and Ray supported him, bringing him to the front door. Liam was limping, moving sluggishly. Inside, a woman was standing in the hall with a tray of medical supplies and bandages. She did not speak but her eyes fell to the blood on Liam's shirt. "The front room," Gabriel said, guiding them in. He lowered Liam onto the sofa.

Gerry came in through the front door and stood in the door-way to the hall. The door slammed behind him, shaking the floor and walls. "I'll ring Dermot," he said. "Where's your phone?"

"In the kitchen," the woman said. She knelt down beside the doctor.

"Thanks."

Ray took a step back. He stood like a voyeur in the room. He felt like he was only an obstruction and stepped further back, moving out into the hall slowly. He heard Gerry's high voice carrying down to him from the kitchen. Then he heard the phone put down on the receiver and Gerry's Doc Martens coming out into the hall.

"You can go on home now," Gerry said.

"Is there anything I can do?"

"No," Gerry said. He stopped in the hall and crossed his arms restlessly. He shifted. "Dermot's on the way."

"Do you know who those guys were?"

"Yeah, I think so." He paused and looked past Ray. "I don't know. Could've been someone else."

"UVF?"

"No," Gerry said. "Stickies."

"Stickies? What does that mean?"

"It means someone's been talking, if it was them. Official IRA. They were waiting for us."

Ray thought back to Michael at the barn. He wondered what Gerry had heard, if anything. "Recognize the car?" he asked. "It was a Saab."

"Ah, it would have been stolen."

Gabriel came out of the room. Ray turned. The doctor's shirt was soaked in blood. He was wiping his hands on a wet towel. "It's not as bad as it looked," he said. "But he's lost a lot of blood."

"He's going to make it?" Gerry asked.

"That he will. The round caught him in flesh he had to spare. Went clean through. Nothing vital hit, by the look of it. Should be taken to a hospital, though."

Gerry shook his head. "You know we can't do that, Gabriel. Wouldn't do."

"I know, lads. You did the right thing bringing him here."

"Go on home now, Ray," Gerry said. "Thanks for your help."

"I'll stick around," Ray said.

"You won't."

"I can help," Ray said. He knew that this was a moment that mattered. A moment of potential immersion, of insertion.

Gabriel shook his head. "Both of you go on home, now," he said. "I have this from here. I'll take care of him and speak to Dermot when he arrives."

"I'll stay on," Gerry said.

"To be blunt, I can't be having ye here. It would do me no favours if the guards showed up."

Gerry stared for a moment and then nodded. "You're right," he said. "Come on, Ray. I'll drive you home."

They went back out to the car and sat inside. Gerry started it and pulled back around the corner. He drove past the house again and began to move through the short, narrow streets toward the center of town.

"You did good today," Gerry said eventually. "I should thank you."

Ray kept his eyes on the stubby, rugged buildings they passed. "There was nothing else to be done."

"Do you care about Ireland?" Gerry asked.

He was silent for a moment. "What do you mean?"

"I mean, do you really care about what we're trying to do? Or, is it all for the money?"

"I care more than I did when I landed," Ray said. "I know you're on the right side."

The light was caught in the glass and the glare spread across it. "Loyalists in the North killed over 500 Catholics in the last three years," Gerry said. "Mostly civilians."

There was a long silence as they continued to drive, moving past warehouses and fenced lots. Eventually, Ray decided to break it. "Why did you join up?" Ray asked.

Gerry hesitated then spoke. "When I was at school, the priest called me into his office and asked me what I wanted out of my life. I don't know why. He might have done it to everyone. I don't remember." He turned the corner. "Do you know what I told him?" he asked.

Ray shook his head and waited—he knew that Gerry would answer himself.

"I told him I wanted to die for Ireland's freedom." Gerry said.

"Is that true?"

"Yeah."

"What did he say?"

Gerry laughed. "He broke my little finger with a ruler and sent me home."

Ray laughed too. "You really want to die for Ireland?" he asked.

"Fuck no," Gerry said, "but I am prepared to do it."

"It's what you've always wanted, then."

"To be an IRA man?" Gerry laughed again.

"No?"

"It's different in the North. Up there, you grow up in a neighborhood and wind up in the youth wing and then just graduate into the ranks. It's the only thing you know. Here, ah … I had to go out of my way. Look, it doesn't really matter now, does it?" There was silence for a while again. Then Gerry looked across. "You really kept it together back there."

"I guess," Ray said.

"You guess?"

"Yeah."

"You've been shot at before?"

"In the army," Ray said.

"You were in the army?"

"Yeah. Vietnam."

"You were in Vietnam?"

"I was."

Gerry shook his head. "So, you've seen combat? Like, real combat?"

"I have."

"This must look small time to you. No wonder you're not fussed."

Ray didn't reply.

"So, you know about this kind of thing, then. Guerilla warfare, I mean. You've fought them."

"I have."

"We study the Viet Cong, you know."

"I don't see a lot of tunnels around here."

"You'd be surprised," Gerry said. "So, what do you think you know about guerillas?"

"I know they beat us," Ray said. "But we were fighting them in their own home so they were always going to win. The more we killed the more there were." They slowed at an intersection and a woman crossed before them. "It's psychological. They don't fight fronts and they don't hold ground. They pick battles they can win and then disappear. Drive fear into the heart of the occupier."

Gerry was silent but Ray could tell that he was thinking so he continued. "All I really know is what it was like to sit out there in the jungle at night in a place you don't know with noises you can't make out filling the darkness around you. I know what it's like to wait. To wonder if, when, they were going to come. If you'd see them or hear them. If the grenade would get you first."

"Did you believe in what you were doing there?" Gerry asked.

"I don't know," Ray said. "You didn't think about it like that. You were there and you had to survive."

"And what do you think now?" Gerry asked.

"I was a kid with a draft card," Ray said. "I don't know what else to say."

They slowed in front of the flat. Ray realized that he hadn't told Gerry where he lived but that they were now sitting in front of the building. Gerry said nothing of it but he knew that it wasn't an oversight.

He got out of the car and closed the door and began to walk up to the door of the building he now lived in. He thought about the lies he had told and the bits of truth in them.

He hoped one day to meet someone who had been in Laos. Someone he didn't know but who knew what he had seen.

Someone who he would never see again so he could speak openly and with candor. Someone who had done horrible things so they would cast no judgement.

He didn't need to look at pictures. He just wanted to talk. Pictures were no good anyway because he could still see it and vision was so little of it at the end of the day. It was the feeling and the atmosphere—the being—and that was something that couldn't be shown. Anyone could look at a picture but feeling was carried within.

He hoped, maybe, to sit out on a porch talking freely with the light on behind the screen door and the empty hum of insects in the dark surrounding. A night that stood still in time. That lasted as long as it needed to and no longer. That was gone forever with the screen door clap.

Chapter 15

Slowey spit over the railing. It was a cold day. The glob of saliva hit the water and then sat there, swirling with the flow of the river. "Jesus," he said. "I'm some glad I wasn't there."

"I'm just lucky he didn't have better aim," Ray said, leaning on the railing, watching the glob roll away and disappear.

"Will he make it?"

"Liam?"

"Yeah."

"Yeah, I think he'll pull through," Ray said.

Slowey shook his head. "That'll teach you, eh?" He turned away from the water and watched a young family pass by on the road. He eyed the father with disgust, then ran his hand through his thin hair, massaging the smooth scalp.

"What do you mean?" Ray asked, eyeing the gangster.

"You need to steer clear of that," Slowey said. "You can't get too close. That shit's for them, not us."

"They're our contacts," Ray said. "That's why we're here."

"You just need a bit of distance. How do you think I managed to stay afloat when everything went down with the boys in Leitrim?" He reached into his chest pocket and drew out the pack of cigarettes. He pulled one out and placed it between his cracked lips.

"It was work," Ray said. "That's why I was there."

"We both know why you was down there, Ray."

"What're you saying, Tommy?"

"I'm saying, that's not what we do," Slowey said. "You want a woman, go find one somewhere else. This can be the easiest job in the world. Just sit back and see that everything keeps running." He tucked the pack back in his pocket and lit the cigarette. "If you get too close, you jeopardize the whole thing."

"That's a big word for you, isn't it?"

Slowey pulled on the cigarette and turned toward Ray slowly. He took it from his mouth and let out a cloud of smoke. "Don't fucking come at me, Ray," he said. "We ain't friends like that. If you start fucking things up, I'll fucking bury you and Bucky'll thank me for it."

Ray looked up into the man's cold hard eyes and wondered how far Slowey would really go if it came down to it. From the corner of his eye, he saw a pedestrian glance their way. "Don't ever threaten me," he said, speaking slowly and quietly.

"It ain't a threat, Ray. That's just the way it is, a fact of life." He ran his tongue over his yellow teeth. "Something like that happens … the police are going to be all over this town for months, you know that as well as I do."

"The police won't get anything from John," Ray said, though he knew that Slowey was right. But, the risk came with reward. He was now closer to the group than ever, working his way in.

"You wanna go get yourself killed in some feud you've got nothing to do with, be my guest. But, you're not gonna take me down with you," Slowey spat. He didn't wait for a response before he turned and started to walk away. "You need anything," he said over his shoulder, "you know where to find me."

Ray stood at the railing and watched the Southie hood cross the street, heading for O'Neil's. Slowey was smarter than he looked, Ray thought. A little distance might not be a bad thing. He was little more than a means to an end, a bridge to cross. They didn't need to be close—not any longer.

Chapter 16

There was a knock at the door early in the morning and his first thought was of police. When he opened the door, Gerry and Dermot were standing in the hallway looking serious. Dermot looked like Liam but bigger and kinder.

"We want you to come with us," Gerry said.

"What's this about?" Ray asked. But they wouldn't tell him. He did not like the men showing up at his flat unannounced in the early hours of the morning. He had done the same thing before himself. He remembered appearing at a hotel room before the sun crested the roofs with a partner of his own to take an agent away in a car. He remembered what came next too.

While he got dressed, they sat in his kitchen at the table beside the window. He went down with them and got into Gerry's car, parked along the curb out front. When they sat down, he saw the butt of the snub nose .357 in the pocket of Gerry's coat. It sat there in plain sight. The gunman made no effort to hide it.

"Where are we going?" he asked.

"Skreen," Gerry said. He spoke without hesitation and didn't glance back over the seat. The car pulled away from the curb and onto the road.

"What is Skreen?" Ray asked. "Is that a place?"

"You'll know when we get there."

They drove out of town and onto the road. Mountains stretched up against the sky like buttes in a spaghetti western. As they drove out towards them, Ray's eyes fell repeatedly to the gun that was protruding from Gerry's pocket. Visions of an execution played through his head. He tried to remain composed—to remember his training. It was difficult now. He regretted getting into the vehicle.

"Someone needs to tell me what's going on," Ray said. "Or I'm jumping out." He wished that he'd left the last part out. It sounded desperate. It demonstrated weakness to them.

Dermot looked at him in the rear-view mirror for a moment, then shook his head, grinning. "Go on," he said, looking to Gerry. "The poor lad is shaking in his boots."

Gerry didn't look in the rear-view. He kept his eyes on the footpath and the narrow streets around them. "We know who did it, and we're going to hit them tonight," he said. "And we want you to come with us."

Ray watched the side of his face, trying to read him. He looked at Dermot too, who revealed nothing. It made him suspicious. They couldn't trust him that much already—it didn't make sense. "Why?" he asked.

This time Gerry looked in the rear-view. His eyes were on the man in the backseat. "Because you've seen enough that we need to know if you can," he said. His voice was steady.

There was no mistaking the implication. It wasn't a threat, really, Ray thought. It was a statement of fact. The car moved through the streets and then out of the town into the countryside. He watched the few familiar landmarks pass along the side of the road.

The countryside grew and fell, and they passed houses, ruins, and fields. The car wound until they reached a small dirt drive pulling away from the road between a cluster of shrubs. Dermot turned up the drive and they began to climb a slight incline, jostling over ruts on the dirt road. A narrow strip of grass tufts ran up the middle.

It grew dark for a moment as the growth around the drive grew up and blocked the sun and then it was light again. After a short while a farmhouse became visible. It sat at the crest of a slight hill among a cluster of outbuildings. Fields stretched out on all sides.

The house itself was two stories, white and squared with a sloping roof. A low white wall ran across the front, separating the small garden in front of the house from the drive. *Misneach* was written on a small wooden sign.

Two sheepdogs ran out from behind the wall, barking in a sharp high tone. They disappeared in front of the car. Ray watched them—were it not for the continued yaps, he would have thought that they'd been hit. Dermot continued to drive, slowing to a halt in front of the house. He parked and shut off the engine.

"There we are," he said. Dermot opened the door and then Gerry did the same. The smell of manure carried through the gap. Ray opened his door as well and followed the men out of the car. The sound of the doors clapping shut echoed across the farm. The barking dogs bounded up and nipped at his ankles.

Dermot and Gerry began to walk toward the house. Ray followed again, glancing over his shoulder. The air was crisp. A red tractor was parked along the side of a barn. The door of the barn was open, and he could see cattle and muck in the darkness. He followed the men up to the side door of the house, moving along a flagstone path.

A pair of mucky green rubber boots stood beside the narrow door. Dermot opened the door and stepped through, wiping his shoes on the mat outside. Gerry did the same. Ray glanced over his shoulder again, looking for anything unusual, and then followed them through. As soon as he stepped through the doorway, into the low-lit hall, the smell of the old farmhouse filled him.

There was a closet across from the door and a rubber mat with wet boots slumped beside it. The two volunteers walked down the short hall and into the kitchen. Ray followed them, keeping his arms at the ready in case he needed to defend himself against an ambush of some kind. He tried to regulate his breathing. He knew that he would stand little chance if they were planning to kill him.

The kitchen was large. John was sitting at a round wooden table in the middle of the room. There was a black garbage bag in the middle of the table and an AR rifle lying across it. "Lads," John said, nodding to the men as they entered. He had a cup of tea beside the rifle. The clock on the wall behind him ticked loudly and slowly.

Dermot walked across the kitchen to the kettle and picked it up. He filled it with water and then turned it on. Gerry pulled out a chair across from John and sat down. "Have a seat," John said, looking at Ray. Ray looked at the rifle on the table and then up at the man across from him.

"What's going on?" he asked.

"Sit down."

Ray hesitated for a moment, then pulled out a chair beside Gerry and sat down. He lay his open hands on the smooth wooden table, looking over the gun at the man across from him.

"Our first language is not our mother tongue," John said, looking at him.

Ray glanced at Gerry and then at Dermot, who was setting cups down on the table in front of them. Neither man revealed anything to him. "What?" he asked, turning his eyes back to John.

"We speak a language of conquest," John said. "Of self-defeat. It's how we do everything. On their terms—by their rules." He turned his cup slowly as he spoke. Ray watched him across the table. "You know, I can remember meeting people who lived through the hunger," John said. "When I was a boy. It was not long ago."

"Why are you telling me this?" Ray asked. "What am I doing here?"

"You have to understand why we're doing this because sometimes that's the only thing that seems to make sense about it." He was watching Ray carefully. "The men who shot Liam were Irish. They were our own. Of our blood and soil."

Again, Ray thought of Aoife and the gig in the country and the man he'd beaten into the muck. "You know who they were?" he asked.

John nodded.

"They were Official IRA?"

He nodded again.

"Bastards," Dermot said. The word came out like a hiss.

"What's wrong with them?" Ray asked. John looked across the table at him for a moment but did not reply. Ray knew more about the OIRA than he let on. They were the reason he was here in the first place, because the Company was afraid they'd align with the Reds. He knew about Seamus Costello and Sean Garland and especially Gerry Foley, but he didn't know what these men thought, and they didn't know that he knew anything.

"They abandoned Catholics in the North," Gerry said.

"What does that mean? What happened?"

"They thought we should move past nationalism," Gerry said. "To them, it's all about class struggle. They want to organize strikes—industrial action."

"They abandoned the war for it," John said. "All our brothers who've died and been imprisoned and tortured. All for nothing. To us, a united and independent Ireland is our first and ultimate goal."

"They think we can win by taking part in the British system," Gerry added. "But, accept the institutions of the state and you've already lost. You're just playing their game."

"We're already colonized," John said. "Our minds and our tongues. We can't afford to give up any more. We'd have nothing left."

The kettle began to whistle and Dermot stood up. He walked across the kitchen and removed it from the heat, then he poured the water into a teapot and put the kettle back. He brought the pot over to the table and set it down, then took his seat again. Steam rose from the spout of the pot.

"They're communists," Ray said, looking at John again. "The Officials?"

John shrugged. "Ah, sure, they're communists but that's not so bad. Some of our best men have been communists. Connolly was a communist. But he stood alongside Pearse and Clarke and Mac Diarmada."

"That's the rising?"

"The rising, aye. But he knew better than the Stickies. And, what did the British do to him for it?" He paused a moment. "They shot him. They shot him first at the GPO and then as he lay dying they arrested him. They took him from the hospital to Kilmainham on a stretcher and brought him out into the yard. He was too injured to stand so they brought out a chair for him to sit on. He was too wounded to sit, so they brought out a rope and tied him to the chair. Only then could they shoot him dead."

"That's enough history, John," Gerry said.

"There's never enough history," John said.

"We've got something important to do." Gerry stood up and reached across the table. He picked up the rifle and tapped Ray on the shoulder. "Come on," he said. "Time to go."

Dermot set his cup down and stood as well. His chair scraped across the floor. Ray didn't stand yet. "What is it that we're doing?" he asked.

"You're going to drive to a house and you're going to kill a man," John said.

The men's eyes were all on Ray. They did not even seem to blink as they read his reaction. He looked from John to Gerry, who nodded slowly. "Dermot's at the wheel and you're going to sit beside him with this rifle," Gerry said. "Alright?"

Ray pushed out his chair to stand. The killing was no concern to him—he had learned how to come to terms with death—but it seemed that the plan was poorly thought out. They were sitting at the kitchen table in a farmhouse with a drunk old man and a rifle. But he also knew that it was not possible to walk away. This was his test.

The men went out to the car together and climbed inside. Ray sat in the passenger seat and Gerry sat behind him. He remembered the feeling of the pistol in the back of his neck the last time Gerry did so. He tried not to show emotion or concern. Dermot started the car and they drove away from the farmhouse.

They went back down to the country roads and made their way through the fields and forests. Gerry soon passed the AR over the seat to Ray, who took it and held it in his lap as they drove. He wondered what would happen if they got pulled over.

The drive seemed to drag on, streetlights licking the windshield as they moved out of the countryside and into the town. The buildings around them ran in neat rows. Cars were parked at the side of the road. They saw no other vehicles on the road itself but lights were beginning to flicker on in windows around them.

Dermot turned onto a side road. He followed it around a bend and turned again, moving into a cluster of semi-detached houses. Dermot slowed in front of the fourth house in the row and pulled to a stop along the side of the road. The lights were on in the lower windows of the house. Dermot and Gerry were both watching it closely.

"How do you know he's going to be home?" Ray asked.

"You're going to stay in the car," Gerry said. "Keep the window down. If anything goes wrong, unload with that cannon." His voice was quiet and cold.

Ray decided that it was not the time to question anything further. They sat parked across the road for forty minutes. A car rolled out of a driveway up the road and passed by slowly. The driver peered through the low light at them but did not stop. After some time, the light flicked on in the hallway behind the front door and then it opened.

The first man who stepped out of the house and onto the stoop was illuminated by the light above the door. He looked skinny and pale, and Ray wondered if it was Michael. He couldn't see him well—he wondered if Michael would have recovered from the beating in time to pull the trigger. But he was out of the light before Ray could identify him.

The gun in his lap felt heavy. His hand was closed around the handle and his finger ran gently back and forth over the little curve of the trigger. The stock felt cumbersome in the little car. The barrel of the gun was pointing down to the floor, running along the length of his leg.

The door shut after a second man stepped out, this one shorter and more muscular. The men were both wearing dark bomber jackets. They walked away from the house, laughing about something, and parted ways as they neared the Cortina in the driveway. The car sat low to the ground and had a broad sloping tail, like an imitation muscle.

The first man went to the driver's door and unlocked it, then opened the door. The second man did the same. They climbed inside and the doors of the Cortina clapped shut. Ray could see the outline of their heads over the seats through the back window.

Gerry stepped out of the car with the handgun and crossed the street. He approached the passenger side of the Cortina. There was a soft breeze and the plume of smoke rising from the round chimney on top of the house was carrying with it, trailing along over the row.

The car started as Gerry reached the passenger side window. He looked quickly back over his shoulder and then stopped walking beside the window. He brought his right arm up and pointed the handgun into the car, barrel almost touching the glass. Without hesitation, he pulled the trigger.

Three dull claps in rapid succession and glass shattered. The car's engine roared and the gears shifted and stalled. Gerry raised the gun a little higher and arched his elbow, pointing into the car through the shattered window. He fired twice more as the driver's door opened. The driver slumped sideways and then hung out through the half-open door, right arm drooping to the rough pavement.

Gerry turned and hurried away from the car, crossing the road at a half jog. He opened the door and jumped inside. Ray looked at the body drooping awkwardly from the vehicle. Before the door was closed, Dermot had the car in gear and moving. He hit the pedal hard and tore to the corner. He turned hard and hit the gas again, leaving the terrace row behind.

Gerry was shaking in the seat. His hands and arms were trembling—vibrating–adrenaline or fear, or more likely both.

There was a look of distance on his face. He was not looking at the other men, just staring out the window. His chest rose and fell, and he suddenly exhaled long and slow. His head tilted down and he blew, releasing, easing.

When Ray looked away from Gerry and out through the window, the car was on a winding country road. They had already left the town behind. Villages in Ireland were fleeting—brief settlements scattered across farmland, connected by a network of winding roads and relations.

They turned onto a dark road and flew across uneven ground. Branches and limbs brushed the windows, scraping and caressing. Gerry was still holding the handgun. His finger was on the trigger and the safety was off. Ray kept a close eye on the gun over his shoulder in the rear-view. The car rattled and shook over ruts.

They drove back out to the farmhouse, headlights a ghostly haze. There were no sirens and there was no chase. The car rolled up the narrow lane to the house. It was dark and the only sounds were tires on the road and insects. The engine shut off and the headlights died, dragging the path in front of them back into darkness.

They sat in the car for a while, staring through the windshield. Cool air was seeping through the poorly sealed doors. Gerry spoke first. "You tell your friends that they've been used," he said. He didn't look at Ray. "That you can vouch for that."

Ray understood. He was no bystander—that was not possible any longer. Gerry had shown him that the guns were being used. Ray had just watched him gun down two Irishmen at home to do it. He nodded but didn't speak.

Dermot took the key from the ignition and opened the door. The static air broke. Gerry opened his own door and stepped out of the car. Ray climbed out as well. The doors clapped shut and their feet dragged across gravel to the front of the house.

John was sitting at the kitchen table with a bottle of Kilbeggan whiskey in front of him when they entered. An old farmer's shotgun was leaning up against the wall behind him, beside the stove. He watched as they entered and seemed satisfied with whatever he saw.

"Wrap the guns and put them away," he said. "I'll put the kettle on."

"Don't bother with the kettle," Gerry said. He crossed the kitchen and opened a cabinet, then brought out another bottle of whiskey. He set it down on the table and then turned to Ray and Dermot. "Give me the guns."

"I left it in the car," Ray said.

Dermot handed Gerry his revolver. Gerry touched him on the shoulder after. "You did well, Dermot."

Dermot didn't answer but nodded and took three glasses from the cabinet and set them down on the table with a quiet clink. Then he sat across from John.

"Bring in some turf, will you?" John said, looking at Gerry. "And we'll light the fire."

"Aye."

Gerry left the room and Ray sat down beside Dermot. John was watching him closely. He was sitting back in the chair at a near slump, with one hand on the surface and the other below, presumably resting on his lap. The thought crossed Ray's mind that he could be holding a gun but he pushed it away—paranoia, nerves.

"Is there nothing to tell?" John asked.

Dermot shook his head once and poured out two drinks. John pushed his glass in and Dermot topped it up too. He capped the bottle and set it back in the center of the table. He lifted his glass and tilted it to his mouth, letting the amber liquid bathe his upper lip. He tilted it further and drained the glass, then set it back down on the table and uncapped the bottle again.

Ray took his own glass and looked into it for a moment. He'd seen it before. Young men who weren't used to combat and some who were but couldn't grow accustomed. He watched Dermot and knew that he could likely turn the man if he needed to—that he was susceptible.

John was watching him too. Ray lifted the glass and looked at the window behind John, which was dark. He could see the very faint outline of green leaves over the wall rocking slowly with the slightly gusting breeze. He tried not to think about the sound of the gunshots too much. It was dull and cold.

Gerry came back inside and sat down at the table across from Dermot. He reached out for the bottle and poured himself a drink. "It's quiet," he said. "Is there no music?"

"The needle's broken on the yoke," John said. He looked from Gerry to Ray. "Gerry tells us you were in the army," he said.

"I was."

"In Vietnam."

Ray nodded.

"You lads made a real mess of that one, didn't ye?" Dermot said.

"I guess we did, yeah."

Dermot didn't say anything more. It fell silent again. The room was poorly lit and somber. The blue silhouette of branches through the window shifted with the small wind. Leaves brushed against the glass, a soft scrape.

Gerry lifted the bottle again and topped up his quickly emptying glass. "Well, it's too fucking quiet, isn't it?" he said.

"Sing us a song then," Dermot said.

Gerry snorted. "Piss off."

"Ray?"

Ray glanced at Dermot, trying to determine whether or not he was being made fun of. He couldn't tell. It was cold in the room, and he rubbed his arms to bade off the chill. Dermot was looking at him seriously—almost without expression. "I wouldn't know anything worth singing," Ray said.

John's low voice came across the table. *"And it's down along the Falls Road, that's where I long to be."* It was quiet and shook but the tone was warm. Ray looked up at him—the older man was staring down into his glass. His eyes were half closed. *"Lying in the dark with a Provo company."*

Dermot and Gerry were watching the old man. They did not speak or smirk—there was nothing but respect on their faces. Something in Gerry's eyes hinted at relief. He joined in quietly, singing along with John. *"A comrade on me left and another one on me right. And a clip of ammunition for me little Armalite."* Soon, Dermot sang too. The tone elevated, lightened.

I was stopped by a soldier, he said you are a swine,
He hit me with his rifle and he kicked me in the groin,
I begged and I pleaded, sure me manners were polite
But all the time I'm thinking of me little Armalite.

Gerry poured out four more generous measures of whiskey as the three men sang. The glasses emptied steadily and the room seemed to grow warmer as the voices filled it.

And it's down in The Bogside that's where I long to be,
Lying in the dark with a Provo company,
A comrade on me left and another one on me right
And a clip of ammunition for me little Armalite.
Sure, a brave RUC man came up into our street
Six hundred British soldiers he had lined up at his feet
Come out, ye cowardly Fenians, come on out and fight
But he cried I'm only joking when he heard the Armalite.

Sure it's down in Kilwilkie, that's where I long to be,
Lying in the dark with a Provo company,
A comrade on me left and another one on me right
And a clip of ammunition for me little Armalite.

Well, the army came to visit me, 'twas in the early hours,
With Saladins and Saracens and Ferret armoured cars
They thought they had me cornered, but I gave them all a fright
With the armour piercing bullets of me little Armalite.

The three voices carried as one and Ray sat and listened to
the song.

And it's down in the New Lodge that's where I long to be,
Lying in the dark with a Provo company,
A comrade on me left and another one on me right
And a clip of ammunition for me little Armalite

Sure, when Tuzo came to Belfast, he said the battle's won,
Said General Ford, we're winning sir, we have them on the run.
But corporals and privates and armoured cars at night
Said send for reinforcements, it's the bloody Armalite

And it's down in Crossmaglen, that's where I long to be
Lying in the dark with a Provo company
A comrade on me left and another one on me right
And a clip of ammunition for me little Armalite.

As he listened, Ray thought about the Irishmen that Gerry
had gunned down. He thought about the shots and the white
flashes in the windows.

PART II

A TIME OF VIOLENCE

Chapter 17

"My soul ruptured," Aoife said. "After that I was empty."

Knobby wrists like bog-oak wrapped around the lamppost, the tarred-and-feathered girl sagged. A sign hung from her limp neck, stilted against the black earth.

Ray put down the tattered photograph and looked at Aoife. "This is your cousin?" he asked. He felt stupid repeating it but he didn't know what else to say. It was hard to believe. "In Belfast?"

Aoife nodded. "That's what I'm telling ye, Ray. You don't understand this world. What you've gotten yourself into."

"Where did you get the photograph?"

"They sent it to us. To my mam in the post."

"Jesus Christ."

Aoife looked at him. They were in her flat talking about things he'd rather not discuss. It was the nature of their relationship now. "Just go home," she said. "Go back to America. Forget about it all."

"I can't."

"Why not?"

"Because I love you," Ray said. He didn't even know if it was a lie anymore.

"You don't mean that."

"I fucking do, Aoife."

"I'm empty Ray. There's nothing here to love. I'm a black hole."

"You aren't."

"I am. I know what I am and don't fucking tell me I'm not." She looked away, at the window where the gentle raindrops were pattering harmlessly against the glass. "Go home. Go back to America."

"I couldn't even if I wanted to."

"Why not?"

Ray shook his head. "The people I work for … they'd never allow it. I was sent here to do a job and I have to see it through."

"Then go somewhere else. Cuba, or wherever else people go to disappear."

"It wouldn't work," he said. "These aren't people you can hide from. If they want to find me, they will."

"If the boys from Belfast can hide from MI5 without even leaving the country you can get away from a few crooks in Hell's Kitchen halfway across the world."

"Aoife, I wouldn't want to go even if I could. I'm here. I love you and this is my fight too."

"You're a fool."

"Maybe I am."

They sat for a while longer at the table beside the window watching the rain fall at its slow and steady pace. Across the road, the droplets were pouring into the river. The surface was alive and it was somehow like watching music at play.

"It was Michael," Ray said. "Wasn't it?"

Aoife looked at him. He could see in her face that he was right. "What do you mean?" she asked.

"You know what I mean," Ray said. "Who shot Liam, who–"

"Don't talk about that," Aoife said.

"It was because of me. Because of what went down at the farm."

"None of this is because of you. What happened at the farm wasn't about you. It's all far bigger than that."

Ray looked back at the water. "What happened between him and Gerry?" he asked.

"It doesn't matter now."

He was quiet for a while. She was right. Whatever it was, Gerry had finished it. But what he really wanted to know was what had happened between her and Michael. He wanted to know if Aoife had caused Gerry and Michael to fall out—if she had led Gerry to gun the man down in his driveway.

They'd known each other three months now. Things had changed between them. They spent time together. They were always together. When he lay at night and she wasn't there, he could feel the presence of her absence. He was tormented by it restlessly. He was tormented in other ways, less by guilt than by the awareness that it could never live on if she found out.

"Be careful, Ray," she said.

"I will."

Chapter 18

"And they went and knocked on Charlie Nash's door. You see, Willie, his brother, was killed on Bloody Sunday. His dad was shot too." Gerry steered slowly around the bend and into the small village center. "They said 'Charlie, if you come along we can win this war.' But, he wouldn't go. He wouldn't pick up the gun."

Muhammad Ali had knocked out Ron Lyle the night before and so they were talking about boxing. They were talking about Charlie Nash and the fighters up North. But, Ray had his mind elsewhere—on the job at hand. "And, these men, they're from Belfast?" he asked.

Gerry nodded. The road bent gently, drawing a tight row of semi-detached storefronts and houses with it. Cars were parked along the curb. Gerry slowed and pulled up into a narrow alleyway leading between two buildings. The car dipped as it climbed over the small lip. It passed between the buildings slowly. Shadows drew briefly across the interior of the vehicle.

They rolled on into a small car park behind the buildings. A red delivery van was parked in the middle. A man and a woman were sitting in the front. They watched the approaching car carefully. He saw the care on their faces even through the windshield.

Ray remembered soldiers walking the length of vans outside government buildings, checking the undercarriage with mirrors. He remembered checkpoints and wires, sweeps and CS smoke. The car slowed and crackled over the asphalt, rolling to a stop in front of the van.

They were in Blacklion, just across the border from the North. A checkpoint ran right through the town and he wondered how the men were planning to carry the guns back across. It wasn't his business, though, and Gerry had told him as much.

The passenger side door opened on the red van. The man swung out and lowered himself down. He closed the door behind him with care. The driver's door opened and the woman climbed out as well. She moved with more grace. She closed the door and moved away from the van.

"Alright. Let me do the talking," Gerry said. Ray nodded and then the Irishman turned off the engine and got out of the car. Ray opened his door and followed him out. The air was cool and they stood just feet from the front of the van. The man and woman walked around the hood and met.

Gerry approached the couple. "Alright?"

"How're ya?"

"No trouble coming across?"

"It'll be the way back that counts," the woman said, smiling.

Gerry smiled in response. "This is Ray. From America."

"You're the fella we've been hearing about," the man said, nodding to him.

Ray didn't respond. He wasn't sure what to say.

"You have them here?" the woman asked, still looking at Gerry.

"In the boot," he replied, tilting his head toward the car.

"Let's have a look."

Gerry and the woman walked around the back of the car and Gerry opened the boot with the key. Ray and the man stood awkwardly together between the two hoods. The man was in good shape and older than Ray had expected. He looked like a shopkeeper or a postman.

After a few minutes, the woman and Gerry came back up along the side of the car and joined them. "Alright, then?" the man asked. The woman nodded. "And the other thing, then," he said.

Gerry glanced at Ray, then back at the man. "What's that?"

"There's something else we need you to do," the woman said. "Come here." She turned and walked around the side of the van toward the back. Gerry followed her. Ray looked at the man, who nodded to him once. Ray glanced back at the alleyway they'd driven through, and then followed Gerry and the woman to the back of the van.

When they reached the back, the woman reached up and grasped the handle on the back door with her right hand, placing her boot up on the back bumper. She pulled the handle and opened the door. The van was long and tall. The inside had a thin wooden bench running the length of the left side.

A young man with medium-length curly hair sat hunched on the bench, looking at the three people standing at the door of the van. He looked uneasy—slightly frightened. He was pale and the skin was baggy beneath his eyes. He twisted his fingers together nervously.

"This is Hugo," the woman said. "He needs a place to stay for a little while."

Gerry looked at Hugo and then at the woman. He nodded slowly.

"Somewhere quiet."

He cleared his throat and then spoke. His voice sounded slightly hoarse. "We have somewhere that will do," he said. "How long?"

She shook her head. "Until it's safe. Someone will be in touch."

"Ok."

"Come on out, Hugo," she said. He picked up a canvas duffel bag, stood, and walked at a stoop to the end of the van, moving slowly and carefully.

The woman moved to the side and Ray and Gerry stepped back. He climbed down from the van. He was taller than he had looked inside. He still looked just as young—younger, even—though his face was hardened.

"How're ya?" Ray said. Hugo didn't respond. He reached up and ran his hand through his hair.

"Let's move the guns and then we'll be on our way," the woman said.

"Right," Gerry said. "Go on and sit in the car if you like, Hugo."

"I'm alright," Hugo said. He spoke with a thick accent that Ray couldn't pinpoint—something Northern. They walked back to the car. Ray and Hugo stopped beside the third man. Gerry and the woman went around to the back and took two large bundles out of the boot. They carried them around to the van and set them in the back.

Gerry came back up to the front of the van. He shook hands with the man and woman and then turned back to Ray. "Let's go then," he said.

Ray nodded and glanced at Hugo. "Get in."

Hugo walked over to the side of the car and opened the door. Ray climbed into the passenger seat and Gerry got back into the driver's seat. He started the engine and backed the car up, then turned it around. He rolled back through the narrow alleyway carefully and pulled back out onto the little road.

Gerry drove out of Blacklion. The sun cut across the windshield. Hugo sat low in the backseat, watching the houses and buildings slowly fade and the countryside emerge. A stone wall ran the length of the road for a while and then disappeared too. None of the men spoke but there did not seem to be silence in the vehicle.

They went right to *Misneach*, the farmhouse. Gerry pulled the car up the long, curving drive and stopped in front of the house. The dogs ran up along the side of the vehicle barking. He opened the door and stepped out into the muck. Ray and Hugo remained sitting in the car. They did not speak.

Gerry went up to the house and stood in front of the door for a moment, then turned and went around the side of the house. Ray saw him looking through the windows as he walked. He moved slowly and carefully. He rounded the house after a minute and then tried the door.

The door was locked but he stooped and took a key from a small flowerpot beside the door, then stood and unlocked it. He went into the house and closed the door behind him. After a few minutes, he stepped back out and walked back over to the car. Ray opened the door and stepped out.

"There's no one here," Gerry said. "Bring him inside. I'll ring Liam."

Ray rapped on the glass with his knuckles and motioned for Hugo to get out of the car. Hugo opened the door and stepped out. He looked over the roof at the farmhouse and back down the drive, past the fields, to the hedges and road below.

"You'll be safe here," Gerry said. "Come on inside."

Hugo and Gerry walked to the door together. Ray leaned on the roof of the car and looked down over the field for a moment.

When he went into the house, Hugo and Gerry were both in the kitchen. Gerry was holding the phone in his hand, listening to the unanswered ring on the other end.

Ray sat down at the table across from Hugo. Gerry hung up the phone and turned to face them. "He must be out," he said. "I tried John too. I'll try again in a few minutes." He scratched his chin. "You alright here?" he asked.

Hugo nodded. "Yeah," he said. "This is fine."

"You'll be safe here," Gerry said. Ray realized that he had not introduced himself to the man and did not know whether or not he should. They were silent for a moment and then Gerry spoke again. "I'll show you the rest of the place," he said. "Ray, try ringing John again."

Ray went to the phone and dialed John's number. He waited and listened to the phone ring. He set it down after a while and called Liam. Again, there was no answer. He set it down. The house was quiet. He lifted the phone and dialed another number. He waited, listening to the white noise and the ring. This time, someone picked up.

"Hello?"

"Aoife. It's Ray."

"Hi, Ray."

He leaned back against the wall. "Aoife, I'm out at the farmhouse with Gerry." He was cautious about saying too much on the phone. "Can you get a hold of John or Liam and tell them to get out here."

"What's going on?"

"It's important," Ray said. "I tried ringing and couldn't get through."

"Are you ok?"

"Yeah, Aoife. Can you just tell them to come out here, please?"

"Yeah, alright," she said. "I'll get a hold of John."

"Thanks," Ray said. "I'd better go, then."

"Alright, goodbye."

He hung up after that. He felt the weight of the pistol in the pocket of his coat then and, for some reason, it suddenly felt burdensome. He slipped his arms out of the coat and draped it over the back of a chair at the kitchen table. He went to the window and looked out to the back garden and the hedge.

Hugo and Gerry came back into the kitchen. "Did you get a hold of them?"

"No. But, I rang Aoife and she answered. She said she'd find them and send them over."

"Alright, then."

Chapter 19

The dogs began to bark. The sound rushed across the front garden to the driveway. Gerry went to the window and looked out. "That's John now," he said. Ray stood up and came to the window beside him, leaving Hugo at the table alone. It was a matter of habit—of security—to know who was approaching before they arrived.

"That's Aoife there beside him," he said.

Gerry turned away from the window. He left the kitchen and went out through the door. He stood on the stoop and watched the car as it drove up to the house and stopped in front. Ray stayed inside and watched from the window.

Aoife was sitting in the car. John climbed out of the car and Aoife got out after. John walked around the hood and then up to the door where Gerry was standing. He walked slowly and with a slight stoop but his very being seemed to carry weight. The men shook hands and then Aoife joined them. She and Gerry hugged and spoke quietly together, then the three came inside.

Ray turned away from the window. Hugo was sitting at the table still. He looked uncomfortable. The footsteps carried down the hall—Ray could hear the grainy dried muck on someone's soles. John came into the kitchen first and Aoife and Gerry followed. He nodded to Ray then looked at the man sitting at the table.

"Will ye excuse us, please?" John said. His voice was steady. "I want to speak with the young lad."

"Sure, John."

Aoife and Ray and Gerry went back outside and then walked down along the drive toward the barns. The air was brisk. The sky was clear and blue. They walked past the corrugated metal and over mucky ruts worn into the earth from fat tractor tires. There were empty barrels and barrels half full of rainwater.

They walked past wrapped bales of hay, the sweet smell lingering with the smell of manure, and stopped in front of a long cattle gate. Gerry unlatched the gate and swung it open. It sagged slightly on the hinges, bouncing because it was light. They passed through and he closed the gate and latched it again behind them.

They walked up past the rest of the metal structures and sheds, leaving the equipment and machinery behind, and they walked up into the fields. The fields rose up toward a line of trees and they walked toward that. On the rise, they could see far to the west, where the sloping green rose and fell. They saw the snaking road and gridlock hedges.

They moved at an unnatural and staggered pace. The ground was soft and the grass was wet. Their feet sank into it as they moved. Cattle dotted a field nearby, white and brown and mahogany and black. The sun was falling a little lower in the sky and it was golden over the leaves.

They reached the line of trees and passed into them and the ground was hard and brown, a tangle of roots beneath them. They spoke a little as they walked but it was infrequent and insignificant. They moved through the trees a little further to where the stone ruins of a small old house rested. They stood among the ruins for a while and walked around it, stepping carefully over stones jutting from the earth.

"What is this place?" Ray asked, looking through an old window at the cold dark interior.

"Just an old house," Gerry said. "Someone used to live here."

"There's no road up here."

"There's houses like this all over Ireland. It's older than the roads."

"Why doesn't somebody tear them down, or do something with them?"

Gerry laughed. "That's long enough," he said. "Let's turn back."

They walked back through the trees out into the field and began to move down toward the house. It sat below in a cluster with the barns and cars and tractor and tools. It was a further walk than it had seemed on the way up and, moving downhill, felt more unsteady.

When they reached the gate below, Gerry opened it again and they passed through. He closed it and latched it behind them and then they moved past the barns again and came out beside the cars. They went back inside and into the kitchen. John and Hugo were sitting at the table still, but they had a bottle of whiskey between them and two glasses with a measure each.

"Hugo's going to stay here a while," John said. "He's a good lad. I knew his uncle, Joe, rest his soul." Gerry took out a few more glasses and they all sat down at the table. John poured drinks for all. "We'll all be staying here a while to keep an eye on him."

"And Liam?" Gerry asked.

"He's alright," John said. "He has things to take care of."

"I have to work, John," Aoife said.

"I rang your mam. She won't be needing you at the shop now." As if it would give some comfort, Hugo nodded in acknowledgement of the fact. They sat and drank for a while and Ray thought of Tommy Slowey, wondering if someone would tell him. John brought out a deck of cards and they played a few games at an easy pace. They spent the evening in the farmhouse and Ray realized that John was concerned about drawing attention by coming and going.

Hugo didn't talk much but seemed to grow comfortable and, before too long, settled in. Over time, Ray learned a little about Hugo. He was twenty years old and grew up in Derry. His uncle had been in the Old IRA and knew John there. He took part in the Civil Rights marches as a child and then when British soldiers appeared on the streets, he joined the Official IRA. At some point, he joined the Provos and began to make bombs.

At dusk, Ray and Aoife went out into the back garden and stood there for a while looking up at the sky where the colors were changing. There was a soft breeze, nearly absent, pushing through the garden as they stood there together. Ray felt the presence of the woman beside him and was glad for it. There were a lot of things that drew him to her, and it was more than just selfish gratification now.

While they were here, he was alone. He did not have the tabloid paper to check for communication or for news of an extraction. He could not contact the Company if he needed to himself. It was one of those times when he was operating in the dark. It was also the moment when he had the opportunity to strengthen his bond with the unit.

A lot of men in the Company were from Connecticut. They had family branches which reached the *Mayflower*. They knew boardmen and judges and lawyers and wore three-piece suits. He was different, in that regard. He was a regular kid from a regular family that struggled to pay bills and get ahead. He didn't start life with a leg up or a trust fund. His fistfights had been in empty parking lots not in collegiate boxing clubs.

The politicians had been saying that a war was brewing for decades. It was only fear of the absolute power they'd unleashed in Hiroshima and Nagasaki that prevented it from unfolding. He knew, though, that the war was already being fought. He also knew that it would never be lost. Russia was nothing to fear. It was brute. They had more power than Russia and they had more intelligence—than Russia and all of its arms.

The difficulty was that the war was fought on all fronts. It was being fought in the jungles and deserts. It was the guerilla warfare that sapped their strength—when they couldn't simply meet force with force and let the bigger man win. And there were the nuclear bombs, the equalizer.

Aoife moved in closer to him and he put his arm around her. He hoped that no one was looking out through the window behind him but felt that the risk was worth it. It was these moments which forged a connection between them most intimately. It was the perception of some chemical or holistic bond–one that transcended.

He'd started his Company training before leaving school. They traced the roots of words, finding linguistic infiltrations. He learned about code and hidden significance by studying sound and form in poetry. He uncovered metrics. It was a certain way of thinking, of seeing what existed beneath the surface.

He turned away from sports and literature and began to focus on foreign policy and Russian history. He read Schlesinger and Kissinger and learned languages. He began to fall in love with the idea of deception. He had a moral compass, always, but first and foremost he believed in pragmatism and progress.

Now he was standing outside an Irish farmhouse with a volunteer while an IRA bombmaker, a fugitive, took shelter inside. He was in the heart of a world that he would never have seen otherwise and had the rare and privileged opportunity to guide history in the right direction. He was more than just a witness; he was an actor.

Chapter 20

There was a bookshelf at the back of the room. It held a few novels and some plays by Sean O'Casey and a collection of stories by Frank O'Connor. It had works by Connolly and Marx and Malcolm X. A turf fire burned and the smell filled the room. Ray and John and Aoife and Hugo were drinking whiskey by the fire.

"In 1920, in a single day, the boys took out fourteen British spies in Dublin and an entire auxiliary company in Cork," John said, finishing his story. They were far into the bottle and Ray couldn't remember what had brought them there. "It was a major blow to the occupation and put the fear of God into the soldiers," he said. "The Brits struck back by firing into the crowd at a match in Croke Park. They killed a dozen men, women, and children." He paused. "It's always been the same."

Hugo had a stutter and always seemed to start his sentences with care. "I-it's the internments that r-really brought me to the Cause." He looked to John. "They ransack our houses, come in with guns, and the detentions ... like Nazis, they are. No trials. No law. Nothing."

"That's it," John said.

"I remember in '68, i-it was like everything changed. People were tired of just sitting down. After so many years of just t-taking it, the whole community was out on the streets. Dockers and factory girls. It was what they done in Selma that shown us the way. And then the RUC came down on us h-harder than they did the b-blacks in America. Tanks and batons and CS gas."

"I've seen it time and time again," John said. "There's no appeasing them. They aren't content even with submission. They need to see the pain—the fear in your eyes."

"I w-walked my best girl home one night when I was still in school, and the soldiers put us at gunpoint on the Strand Road. They kicked me in the b-back of the knees and beat me with batons. Th-they put their hands up her skirt while they did it. And there was nothing I could do."

"Animals," John said. It was half a growl.

"I w-wrote a letter to the paper," Hugo said. He smiled and blushed. "I thought it'd do some good."

"And did it?" Ray asked.

"I-in a way it did. The next week I was walking home, and the jeeps stopped beside me and they put me on the wall again and this time the barrel of the gun was in my mouth. They said they'd k-kill me if they ever saw me again." He looked at John. "I joined the IRA the next day."

They had been there for two days and so far none of them had left. Gerry knew a man named Joe in town who had delivered food and turf and whiskey the day before. Ray was feeling light-headed from the whiskey and the burning turf and he stood up. When he did, it felt as if the blood was rushing to his head. He was disoriented.

"Alright, Ray?" Aoife asked.

"Yeah." He touched his forehead. "I'm just going to step outside for a moment. Get some air."

"I'll come with you," she said.

"Alright," Ray said. Aoife set her glass down on the coffee table and stood up as well. John picked up the bottle of whiskey and topped up his glass. Hugo held his own out and John poured whiskey into it too. Ray and Aoife walked out of the room and went down the hall toward the front door.

It suddenly felt stuffy in the house and Ray was glad for the burst of fresh air when Aoife turned the handle and pulled the door in. He stepped out first and she came after, closing the door behind her. He looked down from the doorway along the stucco walls to the drive, where the cars were parked.

As he did, he started to think about how the complex would look from an aerial view. He'd spent too much time in Laos. He remembered dark pictures of rice fields and villages and military complexes hidden in the jungle. He remembered looking down from helicopters before machine guns opened up on fleeing farmers. He remembered burnt out sites in the aftermath.

The dogs were suddenly at his feet, and he stooped to pet the closest one, a black and white sheepdog with medium length hair. The eyes were black and soft. She was named Prince, he'd learned. She was old—older than anyone could remember. Her teeth were yellow and long. The hair was rough and stiff because she spent her days outdoors and in the fields chasing mice and rabbits.

Aoife was watching him with the dog and he stood up and looked at her and she smiled. "Did you ever think you'd be here, Ray?"

He smiled too, then. "No," he said honestly. "I didn't."

"It's a strange old world, isn't it?"

"It is."

She was wearing a green dress and it made her eyes something powerful. They walked down to the corner of the house and he put his right foot up on the short wall and leaned forward on his knee. It felt awkward and he took his foot down but they stayed standing there for a while looking at the barns and the field and the trees and road below.

"He seems alright, doesn't he?" Ray asked.

"He does," Aoife said. "You think you know poverty and oppression until you've been to the Bogside."

"You've been?"

"I have."

"And what's it like?"

"Shite," Aoife said.

Ray smiled. "That's a word you don't hear in America."

"Shite?"

"Yeah," he said. "It's a funny word."

"You're pissed," Aoife said.

"That's another."

"You don't say that there?"

Ray shook his head. "No. And if you do it means something else."

"Will you take me there someday?" she asked.

"America?"

She nodded.

"Yeah." He turned and looked at her. "When this is all over."

Aoife gave him a weak smile. "I don't think it ever will be."

Ray looked at her for a long time and didn't reply. He was thinking about Nelson and the Company. Then his eyes fell to her chest, and he was thinking about what she looked like naked and he was glad that he'd wound up in Sligo. He felt bad, too, but he tried not to think about that. "Are you going to sleep in my room tonight?" he asked.

"Yeah," Aoife said. "And you'll wake up with a bullet in the head and Gerry standing over you."

Ray laughed. "There are worse things could happen."

Her smile faltered. "You don't mean that," she said, though they both knew that he did. It was a hard world and sometimes it felt like there was no time for love.

"Where is he, anyway?" Ray asked.

"Gerry?"

"Yeah."

"I think he's in his room," Aoife said. "He finds it hard to be around people too long."

"Why's that?"

Aoife shrugged. "He's always been that way. Since we were children."

Ray nodded. "He's a good guy," he said. He meant it too.

"He is."

They stood there a little while longer, not talking, and just enjoying the quiet. Crickets or some other form of life made quiet chirps in the grass or the trees somewhere and other than that it was just the sound of the earth. Aoife came closer and he turned and kissed her and then they stood there, side by side, just touching.

It was nice, he thought, to feel the comfort of another. It was bitter too to have a slight taste of something that was not his and would never be. He didn't mean Aoife but the whole thing. With Aoife, it was bitter for another reason too, and that was because he knew that it was artificial and would eventually go away.

"Should we go back in?" he asked, because the peace had come to an end and the quiet was suddenly a burden.

"Yeah," Aoife said, looking back at the house. "I reckon we should."

"Alright," Ray said. He stooped to pet the dog again and he felt the bristly fur against his fingers and palms. He stayed with it for a moment, letting the heat of the animal warm his skin, and then he stood and walked back up toward the door. Aoife walked with him.

Ray opened the door and stepped through. Aoife came behind him. She shut the door. The smell of turf was in the house and the heat was stifling. He could hear the voices of the two men, the two soldiers, in the other room. He wished they'd stayed outside a while longer but he knew they would have heard the door and couldn't turn back.

They went back down the hall and into the front room. "Alright?" John asked, looking up when they entered.

"Yeah," Ray said.

Hugo was holding the bottle. It was nearing the end. "You'll have another?" he asked, tilting it.

"Yeah," Ray said. "Give us another there."

"There's a good man."

Chapter 21

There was a crackle of tires. He opened his eyes, and the blue light was coming through the window. His head was still spinning from the drink. He heard movement somewhere toward the back of the house. A sudden rush of footsteps carried down the hall. They were heavy.

Ray sat up quickly and looked at the door. The door burst open. His vision sagged. Aoife rushed in with an AR rifle in her hands. "Get up!" she hissed. "The army's here."

"Jesus Christ." Ray threw his legs over the edge of the bed and stood up quickly. His head rushed. He grabbed the jeans that were thrown over the dresser and pulled them on. Aoife handed him the rifle and then leaned down and picked up another one, which she had leaned against the wall outside the room.

Ray took the gun from her. He stood, bare chested and barefooted, with the rifle in his hands and looked at Aoife. She was wearing a sweater and a dress, and he wondered when she had had time to put on clothes. "What now?" he asked.

"We have to go." She turned and ran down the hall toward the stairs. The moonlight was coming through the window, spreading up the wall. Ray followed. They reached the end of the hall, and he heard two vehicles roll up in front of the house. The sound of the tires on the loose stones was grating.

Gunshots ripped through the night—an automatic weapon firing in the field behind the house. The sound was devastating. Ray jumped. "Fuck!" Aoife spun. Her face was white, scared. There was panic in her eyes. "John took Hugo out the back door," she whispered. "That'll be them."

"Come on!" Ray said. He grabbed her and pulled her away from the stairs. Gunshots tore back, a return of fire. As he ran down the hall toward his room, he heard a window shatter downstairs and even louder bursts of gunfire coming from the front of the house. Wherever Gerry was, he must have been shooting too. There was too much gunfire otherwise.

They reached the bedroom, and he ran to the window overlooking the back garden. He shifted the rifle to his left hand and unlatched the locks, then began to wind the handle, opening the window. It squeaked quietly. "Just break it!" Aoife hissed. There were footsteps downstairs, soldiers sweeping the house.

The window was open. "Go," Ray said. "Drop clear of the house and roll. Then run to the trees. Don't look back."

There was another steady burst of fire. The cracks echoed. Aoife looked out the window and then dropped the rifle. She climbed through and turned, dropping herself as carefully as she could. There was a shrub beneath the window and she landed in it. Branches snapped. There were steady, quiet footsteps coming up the stairs.

Ray tucked the rifle beneath his bicep and climbed out the window, dropping into the shrub. He landed with his back. Branches dug into his skin, and he rolled off the shrub to the ground. Aoife was picking up her gun. "Run!" he whispered. She took off across the back garden, and Ray did too.

They made it half-way to the trees and a single shot rang out from the window. For a second, he expected to see Aoife jolt forward and hit the ground. But she continued to run and the shot was followed up by another sharp burst. Ray spun and pointed the rifle in the general direction of the window and squeezed the trigger, unleashing a series of rounds at the house.

He turned hard and continued to run to the trees. Aoife made it before him. She moved through the branches, and he came after. She looked over her shoulder. "Keep going," he said. "Don't stop." They ran together through the trees, light cutting through the limbs, stumbling over roots and around branches. The trees cleared and they entered another field.

The sky was clear but for a few light clouds. The moon hung above and the stars around it danced. Ray was breathing hard and was beginning to shiver from the cold. He felt goosebumps on his arms and chest. "Where's Gerry?" he asked.

"He went after John and Hugo," Aoife said. "I think he was out of the house before us."

"Where are they headed?"

"Thomas O'Shea's."

"You know how to get there?"

Aoife nodded. "But it's back that way. Down the road."

"Let's keep moving," Ray said. "To the trees ahead, the other side of the field. We'll get to O'Shea's when we can." They continued across the field. Ray felt the cold wet ground against his feet. They began to hurt. He felt the hard ridges of the gun against his bare skin. There was no more gunfire from the house, and he knew that the men had either escaped or had been killed.

John was not young, but he had been through combat, it seemed. Ray knew that intelligence and experience was enough sometimes. He found himself hoping that John had made it, both for his own selfish purposes and because he felt an affinity with the man now. It was a strange sensation being in Ireland. In Laos, there was a frame of warfare around his actions. Here, it was not quite as solid. He lived in a liminal zone.

Barefoot and bare chested with the rifle in his hands, trudging through a cold mucky field, he could not help but think back, even as he ran for his life. He wondered if Aoife had ever seen anything like this before. He had once imagined that all the volunteers were versed in bombing and shooting but he was not so sure now.

They slowed by the time they reached the tree line. They carefully stepped over a barbed wire fence running along the edge of the field and made their way into the trees again. The soldiers would be searching for them. Ray felt the branches scraping his shoulders and back and stooped low to move beneath larger limbs.

The muck caked his feet and spread between his toes. The cold wet grass licked at them too. The stumps and roots were gnarled and rough. His feet were scraped and cut. The sky was growing lighter overhead, though it was still in the earliest stages of morning. Ray realized, then, that he had no sense of the time and true uncertainty struck for the first time. Uncertainty—fear.

He was in the woods with a rifle and a revolutionary. He had no shoes, no shirt, and no safeguard. He thought about Nelson. Nelson was recruited by the old guard, Paragon, an OSS codebreaker who taught at Yale. He was calculating and pragmatic, a true Company man. The Company couldn't—wouldn't—rescue him here. With the *New York Times* and the Family Jewels scandal, the Company wouldn't want to risk anything. Leaks about Lumumba and Castro were enough. They would rather he die. He was on his own in Ireland and things were beginning to turn against him.

They walked for a long time and moved from trees to fields and eventually reached a hill from which they could see a small road below, which they walked parallel to for a while. They both had their guns and Ray was conscious of his appearance. He knew that the soldiers would not easily give up the search but also knew that the soldiers were likely not meant to kill in Ireland—they were likely not even meant to be in the Republic—and would not likely spend much time in the fields.

After a while, he realized that Aoife was crying silently, and he pretended not to notice. He felt like crying himself because he was nearly naked in the cold and wet and was beginning to wonder why he was here. He continued to walk because that was the job of soldiers and because above all else he knew to persevere.

Aoife stopped walking and he looked at her and realized that she had reached a wall. He stopped too and looked back across the field. All he saw was the sloping hill and the trees and the glisten of dew on the leaves and the grass. He felt the cool air and he looked down at the ground and then sat, setting the rifle down in the grass beside him.

The water seeped through his jeans, and he began to feel itchy and coarse. Aoife sat too. She set her rifle down beside her and leaned against him. He put his arm around her, and she leaned in further. They sat looking down at the road below and no cars passed. The stars were out and the moon was nearly full.

Ray lay back against the hill and Aoife came with him. They looked up at the stars and he felt her head on his chest as he breathed. Her hair was in fine strands that separated. Her cheek was cold and wet. He ran his hand through her hair as they lay there and tried not to think about the soldiers that were coming for them.

Not moving, he began to grow colder. He was shivering soon and Aoife burrowed into his chest and tried to warm him. He raised his left hand, which was free, and looked at the fingers. They trembled. "We should keep going," Aoife said, lifting herself with her arms and looking down at him.

"Are you ok to go on?"

"Yes," she said.

"Ok."

They sat up and picked up their rifles, then stood. The guns were damp from the grass. Ray's fingers began to grow numb as he held the rifle, but he knew better than to let it go. Aoife smoothed out her sweater and brushed the loose grass from it. "Should we start going toward O'Shea's?" she asked.

"Can you take us there without going back to the farm?"

Aoife looked around and then nodded. "Yes," she said. "I think so."

"Ok then. Let's go," he said. They started off again, still walking parallel to the road. This time, Ray allowed Aoife to lead the way. Now that he was following, and the adrenaline was wearing thin, he began to slow. He felt uneasy. It was cold.

"It's not far," she said. "But it might take a while to get there."

"That's ok."

"Are you alright?"

Yeah," he said. "Just keep moving."

Chapter 22

Thomas O'Shea's farmhouse stood alone on a hill looking down a sloping drive to the road. The walls were white and there was blue trim around the windows. A fence ran the length of the property along the road. It met a line of shrubs which divided the O'Shea property from the next field. There were lights on in the house, but all the curtains were drawn and so the yellow light was muted through them.

"That's it there," Aoife said. They stood in the middle of a neighboring field looking at the house. Their feet and ankles were caked in muck. Their fingers were cold and stiff. The guns were growing heavy in their hands. "What do you think?"

"I think we have little choice," Ray said.

Aoife exhaled. Her breath hung in the air, then dissipated. "Ok."

"We need to be careful. They could be waiting for us here. They could've followed John. Or caught him."

"He wouldn't give us up," Aoife snapped.

"Torture will do funny things to people," Ray said. He began to move across the field toward the house and Aoife walked with him.

In Laos, Ray had spent most of his time in towns and cities. He rode in jeeps and helicopters. Sometimes, though, he had to go into the brush and fog and trails, where there were men bunkered down with grenades, where politics and morality did not matter, and where everything was a matter of self-preservation and survival and fear.

They climbed over the fence and moved closer to the house with the moon hanging low in the sky above. He kept his eyes moving across the field and the road and searched for any movement or light or flash of metal. His finger nestled on the trigger of the gun. He saw nothing that was not meant to be there. It was quiet and still.

There was a time when he'd been in the brush and men began to come through the hot fog and onto the trails. He remembered the sudden and instant breach—the stillness that previously sat so eerily over them was shattered with the rattle of gunfire and the bursting of grenades. There was a rush—feet and bodies. He'd hit the ground and held his pistol close and made his way to the shelter of trees as the soldiers clawed one another desperately for survival.

Aoife stumbled beside him and his arm shot out to catch her. He grabbed her elbow to help her stand, though the motion was jarring and tugged her arm in the socket. She winced and straightened and smiled weakly at him.

"You ok?" he asked.

"Yes."

They continued to walk and the house was drawing closer. They moved around the back and began to walk slowly. Strange things happened to men in war. The strangest things seemed to happen to the Americans but maybe he thought that only because he understood them the best and so it seemed all the more unusual when he didn't.

When men were seeped in sweat and urine and muck and the smell of gunpowder and chemicals was around them it did something to them. He saw reasonable intelligent men–boys sometimes—begin to stalk one another, begin to harbor murderous grudges, over the most insignificant perceived slights. He heard stories more than he saw it.

He wondered whether or not Gerry could be trusted. That was what it came down to. He had been thinking about Gerry and his absence and the SAS raid, and the fact that he'd been sleeping with Aoife. Gerry hadn't seemed to care but now that Ray was cold and wandering half-naked in the night, he began to wonder if a trap lay ahead, if the Irish had some version of an honor killing and if he and Aoife were to die.

They reached the back of the house and he tried to peer through the windows but the curtains were all drawn well. He tried to listen at them but could hear nothing from inside. He was trembling and Aoife was standing beside him looking as frightened as he felt. "We just have to do it, don't we?" he asked.

Aoife nodded to him. "I think so," she said. He wondered, if John and Gerry were there, why they were not keeping watch and had not seen them coming. And, if they had seen him and Aoife coming, why they had not given them some sign—some peace of mind.

They rounded the corner, moving carefully, and walked up to the back door of the house, beside what must have been the kitchen. Ray tapped on it softly with the barrel of his rifle. He waited for a moment in the suspended silence and then rapped harder, this time with the butt of the gun. He regretted that immediately and began to imagine a shotgun blast tearing through the door in response.

There was a shuffling noise and then the door opened a crack. It was dark in the hall on the other side but an old woman was standing there looking at him. Her eyes took in his bare chest and dirty, scratched face, and the rifle in his hands. They then moved to Aoife, who was standing behind him. The woman stepped back and opened the door wide.

"Elizabeth," Aoife said.

"Aoife. Come in, dear."

Ray stepped through first and then Aoife came after. "Thank you," he said to her as he entered.

"Not at all," Elizabeth said, her voice soft and genuine. "This door is always open to those who serve the Cause."

Ray stopped in the hall among coats hanging from hooks and rubber boots and walking sticks. The house was warm and cozy. His feet were wet against the ground. He was shivering.

"Put that gun down," Elizabeth said, "and let's get you into a bath."

"Eli—"

"Get those wet clothes off you, Aoife. I'll run the bath and then get you something warm and dry." Elizabeth closed the door. "The men are in the other room. Thomas and John and Gerry."

At that moment, John appeared through a doorway at the other end of the hall. "They killed Hugo," he said. "A sniper put him down through the trees."

Chapter 23

"It had to be Joe," Gerry said. He was looking at John from the sofa in the sitting room. John was standing beside the doorway. Gerry lit the cigarette he had between his lips and threw the match into the ashtray on the small round table beside the sofa. It smoldered and bent and blackened.

"I was thinking the same thing," John said.

Ray looked at Aoife, who was wrapped in a blanket on the sofa beside Gerry. "Who gave us up, you mean?" he asked.

"Who else could it have been?" John asked. "It wasn't Liam or Dermot. I can tell you that."

"No," Gerry said. "It wouldn't be either of them."

"And everyone else who knows is here," John said. "Even the command don't know where we were staying."

Aoife pulled her knees up onto the sofa. Gerry looked disappointed that nobody had contradicted him—that nobody had come to Joe's defense. Ray was impressed that Gerry had been the one to say it. That he hadn't backed down from it. He remembered, again, the time that Gerry had pressed a gun against his head, ready to pull the trigger.

"Does it make sense?" Ray asked. They looked at him. "For Joe to do it."

Attention turned to Gerry again. Elizabeth had disappeared from the room, but Thomas was sitting silently in the corner. He was picking at his nails, as if unconcerned and unaware of the conversation at hand. Aoife lifted her head and looked at her cousin. "You've known him a long time, Gerry," she said. She didn't say more and didn't have to.

Gerry shook his head. There was pain on his face. But when he answered it was in the affirmative. "I have indeed known Joe a long time." He paused a moment, looking down at his boots. "It had to be him. He's a good man but he's weak." He hesitated again. "He's been in trouble before too. Drugs."

Like that, there was a collective nod. Ray knew that a judgement had been made. A sentence would be passed. He wondered if it really had been Joe. It was claimed that MI5's penetration of the IRA was sophisticated enough to read the minutes of command meetings before half the senior ranking men. But, if Joe was in the crosshairs, he wasn't.

"I'd say it's never the ones you think but it often is just that," John said. Thomas gave a deep grunt of agreement. It was the first time he'd weighed in on the subject. It was the full extent of his opinion too, it seemed. He didn't look up from his nails. John leaned forward. "Give Liam a ring, will you?" he asked.

"Oh my God, they don't know yet," Aoife said.

"Sure," Gerry said. "That alright, Thomas?"

"Ask Elizabeth for the telephone," Thomas said. "It's in the kitchen."

"Thanks," Gerry said. He stood and left the room. They listened to his footsteps carry down the hall to the kitchen and then the low sound of his voice speaking to Elizabeth. They sat for a while, not speaking much.

After a short time, Gerry came back down the hall and stepped through the doorway. His face was white. "I rang but couldn't get through..... I got a hold of Dermot," he said. He spoke with hesitancy. "Liam's been arrested. They raided his flat. They found a gun."

"Ah, Jesus," John said. He put his head down, looking at the ground. "That's it for him."

Aoife took her feet down off the sofa and looked around. "What's happening?" she asked. "Is this it?"

"Ah, shut up," Gerry said.

"Whoa!" Ray said.

Everyone turned to look at him. "Have something to say?" Gerry asked. He looked ready for a fight, then calmed quickly. "No, you're right," he said. "I'm sorry, Aoife."

Aoife shrugged. "What now?"

"Dermot's coming out. I told him where we were."

"Good," John said. "We should all be together now."

They ate dinner soon after that and then sat back in and watched television. They talked little. Thomas talked to John about hurling. Then Elizabeth read for a while and Thomas fell asleep in his chair.

Dermot arrived an hour later. They heard the engine and the tires and saw the long sweep of the headlights. He pulled the van up beside the house and left it parked there. Elizabeth let him into the house and then he spoke to Thomas for a while, who it seemed he knew well.

Thomas and Elizabeth went to bed after that and the rest of them sat in the room and talked about the raids. They kept their guns with them. Dermot thought that Liam was going to be in prison for a long time, he said. It would do him no favors recovering from the gunshot. Gerry told him that Joe had betrayed them to the army or the guards, and that the SAS had killed Hugo. He also said that he thought he'd hit one of the soldiers when he opened fire on the house and John told him that he'd better not have left any bullet holes in the wall.

It soon became clear to Ray that a decision was being made as to what to do about Joe. He had Hugo's death to answer for and Hugo had been handed into their care. He was a volunteer—now a martyr. He had been made their responsibility. That was something they were aware of too. Ray did not speak much. He sat and listened as the group slowly worked toward vocalizing what they all knew was going to happen.

Eventually Gerry said that they would have to question him to find out what the police and army knew. John agreed. He told them to do what they needed to do but not to bring Joe back to the house. Soon after, he went to bed. Dermot and Gerry and Aoife and Ray sat and smoked cigarettes and began to formulate a plan.

Chapter 24

The street was dim blue with the early morning light. Streetlights cast a series of amber halos which faded into darkness. Ray sat in the back seat with the Armalite across his lap, his breath hanging in the air whenever he exhaled. He rubbed his hands together for warmth, the whisper of waves in the distance.

This was an island under siege. It always had been. Sea swell brought ships of conquest, violence, and extraction. At times, it was perverse and primal. At other times, it was deliberate, calculated—implanted, cultivated. Pleasure, pain, possession, and power. Bloodlust.

The late-night frost was fading with the cool morning rise. The window was cracked an inch and air filtered in. He wrapped his right hand around the cold handle of the gun. The left rested on the forestock. In the passenger seat, Gerry railed a line of speed off the dash. He pinched and rubbed his nose, then pulled the balaclava back down over his face. They all wore balaclavas: Dermot, Gerry, Aoife, and Ray.

"Let's do it before this gack wears off," Gerry said. He grabbed the handle and opened the passenger door. He stepped out with the rifle at his waist and started to move around the hood of the stolen van. Ray saw him cross the blue light through the windshield. Aoife opened her door and then Ray did too.

His boots were solid on the ground beneath him. He was aware of it.

Gerry was up on the footpath. A hand-painted sign on the low wall said Longphort. Gerry opened the gate. The squeak of the hinges edged into the night. Ray was aware of the engine of the van rumbling violently along the curb. The growl of a caged and waiting animal.

Gerry was moving up the pathway between the uncut grass and weeds working up through cracks in the concrete. The lights were off in the house. Dull pink curtains were pulled across the windows, matte. When he reached the door, Gerry stepped to the side.

Aoife stepped up to the door and let the rifle fall to her side on the sling. Ray watched the lines of her body beneath the turtleneck and camo trousers as she stooped to the lock and inserted two small metal bars into it. The seconds seemed to stretch on as she picked it. The near silent scrape of the tools carried in the night.

He turned and looked up the road. It was still. The tranquil domestic lull. Dermot was in the driver's seat looking across the front yard, frightened, nervous. There was a latch, then Aoife was standing back and the door was open. Gerry slipped through the black gap and entered the house with his rifle raised. Aoife went through next. Ray followed behind, pushing the door as he passed through and raising the rifle.

It was dark. There was an unidentifiable odor in the air. Not unpleasant—laundry detergent or soap. For some reason he hoped, then, that no old people lived here. His eyes adjusted to the light as he followed Aoife down the hall, the floor creaking beneath their feet. The house was like so many others in Ireland, Ray thought—the layout familiar, built with the cottage in mind.

Gerry stepped into the kitchen as the light came on. There was a strangled gasp and he stopped moving. Through the doorway, he could see Gerry's back and the butt of the rifle against his shoulder. "On your knees you fuckin' cunt."

A pleading woman's voice. "Please …"

"Not another word."

Aoife entered the kitchen. Ray followed close behind. The woman was kneeling on the tile floor, nightdress draped like a gentle caress. She was a little older than he was. Still young. Her hair was tangled, messy. Her eyes were large and panicked, fearful. Her hands were clutched in front of her and she was looking up at Gerry and Aoife. More at Aoife when she recognized that she was a woman.

"Where's Joe?" Aoife asked. Her voice was soft.

"I don't know," the woman said. It was a plea. There was a sound in the bedroom behind the woman. The door was open and the room was dark. Gerry moved past the woman with the rifle raised. "No!" she screamed, she turned and grasped desperately at Gerry's leg.

"Don't!" Aoife yelled. She took a step toward the woman and pushed the barrel of the rifle against her back. The woman shuddered, gasped, but did not speak. She stayed crouched on the floor with the bend of her spine showing through the fabric of the nightdress, bare knees against the tile.

There was a shout of confusion in the other room. The sound of rushing feet. "Who the fu–" The voice was cut by the dull, thick slap of the rifle butt connecting with his skull. There was another noise as the man fell. Then there was silence.

The woman on the floor let out a strangled sob: "Oh my God …"

"Ray, get his feet!" Gerry called from the other room. There was a sudden silence around them. Ray looked down at the woman on the floor, wondering if she had heard the name. Aoife was looking at him with panic and distraught contemplation in her eyes. The woman turned her head and looked up at him from the floor.

Transformations occurred in a matter of seconds. She looked at him with sudden recognition of his humanity. His name somehow contained it. They realized that everything had altered irreparably. There was new fear, even more overwhelming. A stillness. She saw that his reaction was not violent or impulsive. It was contemplative, reflective. Regretful. She knew that a logical response was worse than impulse here. It could lead to only one place.

"Get up," Aoife said, quietly. "You're coming too."

"I didn't hear anything," the woman whispered.

Ray went into the dark room with anger. At Gerry. At himself for making the choices that led him here. The man was lying still on the ground, bleeding from the forehead. His white belly was hanging out under his t-shirt. Gerry was grabbing at his shoulders, trying to lift him. Ray let the gun fall to his side and stooped. He grabbed the man's ankles, disgusted by the cold skin, the hair and bone.

The man began to kick. He twisted and struggled, turning his head. "What the fu–"

Gerry dropped him and his shoulders hit the carpeted floor, followed by the back of his head. Ray let go of his ankles and his heels hit the floor, too, with a single dull thud.

"It's him?" Ray asked.

"Yeah," Gerry said.

Joe tried to sit. Ray grabbed his gun and raised it. He pointed the barrel and looked down the sights. "Just get up and come with us," he said. His finger was in the curve of the trigger. The order sounded more desperate than he had intended it to but when Joe looked down the barrel at the masked man on the other end, he slowly began to rise to his feet.

Ray took a step back. When Joe was standing, Gerry pushed him forward. Ray turned and went back out into the kitchen. He could feel the cold air from the open door down the hall. Aoife was standing beside the doorway to the hall with her rifle in one hand. The woman was standing beside her, resigned.

"We need to go," Aoife said.

"We're done," Ray said. "He's coming."

Aoife nodded. "Go on then," she said to the woman. "Down the hall. Don't cause a fuss."

Gerry and Joe came through the doorway. The woman looked at them. At the blood running down her husband's forehead. There was pity in her eyes. There was also disgust at whatever he had done to put them in this position. She turned and went down the hallway slowly. Aoife walked behind her. Ray let Gerry and Joe pass through the door and then followed them out.

They went down the hall and left the house. Ray closed the door behind them. He looked up and down the street. It was quiet, still. The first few lights were coming on in houses along the row. The van was idling along the curb. Dermot watched from the driver's seat as Aoife led the woman up to the side of the vehicle.

Ray went around to the back of the van and opened the rear doors. Gerry and Aoife loaded the man and woman into the back of the van and climbed in after. He closed the doors over behind them and went around to the front passenger seat. He climbed in and shut the door. Dermot looked at him for a moment, then shifted and pulled away from the curb.

They drove through the neighborhood, past hedgerows and walls and gardens. The lights came on in more houses. Curtains were drawn. The sky was growing lighter overhead. Ray pulled his balaclava off and tossed it on the seat behind him. Dermot did the same, pulling it off with one hand and holding the wheel with the other. There was silence from the back. The stench of panic.

Ray thought about the woman and her part in this. He thought about human nature—about what was natural and what was fostered. The savagery of civilization. Ruthless compulsion. He thought about the boy in Laos, his part in it—more than turning a blind eye—pulling the trigger, in spirit, in effect. He thought about hidden yearning. The ache for power, for release. For violence. The guilt-ridden shameful aftermath. Emotion. Suppression. The cultivation of the ache. The pursuit of blood's quenching force.

There was no ache for blood in the van as it moved through the early morning streets. It was cold, quiet, and frightened. But, he thought, he sat with an Armalite in his lap and two prisoners in the back of a stolen van. That he'd worked his way in was beyond doubt. If nothing else, he'd done his job. For the Company—for America.

Chapter 25

The sun was rising over the hedges as the van moved along the country roads. They drove through the unfamiliar network again, pushing deeper and deeper into the tangle of fields and farms and fences. The air was taut. Ray could hear the stifled whimpers of the captives in the back.

They drove until they reached a small cottage nestled behind a row of overgrown trees. Dermot pulled the van through the gate and parked it in front of the cottage. The building was dark and still, the glass foggy with dust. He sat for a moment with his weathered hands on the steering wheel, looking at the old house, before he turned off the ignition.

Ray opened the door and stepped out of the van with the AR in his left hand. His feet touched the earth and the strap fell down and hung beside his leg. He walked along the side of the van. It was early still and the birds were beginning to sing in the distance. Insects were alive around them. The air was fresh and dewy.

The back door of the van opened and Gerry and Aoife climbed out. The man and woman sat against the wall of the van with pillowcases over their heads, hands bound together. Gerry ground the dirt beneath his feet with the toe of his Doc and then spat. He looked at the gap in the trees leading to the road.

"Let's get these two in the house," he said, looking at Aoife. She nodded. Neither wore their balaclava anymore. Both were pale. The sun was coming up behind the trees and the golden light was coming through the gaps in the leaves and branches.

Aoife climbed back up into the van. The prisoners made no effort to fight or argue as she helped them to their feet and guided them to the back of the van one at a time. She moved Joe first and helped him step down from the van with care. Gerry took him by the arm and gave support. When Joe's wife was down as well, Aoife climbed out of the vehicle and shut the door.

Ray walked back up around the van to the driver's window. Dermot was still sitting at the wheel. He was staring blankly through the windshield at the light in the trees. Ray tapped on the window softly and waved. "Come on," he said. "Inside."

Dermot looked at him for a moment and then opened the door. He stepped down and shut it behind him. His eyes fell to the rifle and he shifted uncertainly. Ray put his right hand on Dermot's shoulder and looked him in the eye. Dermot's shirt was damp. He nodded slightly.

Gerry and Aoife had started to lead the two captives up to the cottage. It was a small old-style Irish cottage with white walls caked in lime and a roof that had been replaced once twenty years before. Dermot locked the van and then the two men followed the others up to the house. Ray was conscious of every footstep that carried across the small drive.

Aoife unlocked the door of the cottage and went inside. Ray walked to the right around the cottage, moving through the long damp grass, to the corner of the building. He turned and went around the side. There was a small garden at the back and another row of trees behind the house, enclosing it.

It was quiet as he walked around the back, looking for anything out of the ordinary. The birds were still singing and they seemed even more present now that he was alone. He could feel the dew working through his shoes and dampening his socks and toes. He shifted the gun into his right hand because it was growing heavy.

The tangle of trees at the back of the house was low but covered them well. The leaves were dense and the branches were many. The trunks were thick and sturdy. There was a low barbed wire fence running along the bottom of the trunks. He wondered who had erected it and why. There must have been animals at one time, but he could not imagine them in the garden.

When he rounded the corner again, he could see the gap to the road. It was quiet and still. No cars had passed since they arrived and they had seen very few on the road in. He walked around to the front of the house again. Everyone else had already gone inside. The door was closed. He looked over to the van.

For a moment, he wondered if the keys were in the ignition. He thought, momentarily, of getting into the van and driving away. He'd been meant to smuggle guns, not commit murder. But, the country was small and enclosed. There was nowhere for him to go. He knew that he never would, anyway. It was simply a momentary thought—a fragment.

Ray walked up to the front door and turned the handle with his left hand. He stepped into the cottage. He was standing in the small kitchen. Dermot sat at the round table in the middle of the room. A set of stairs led up to a short second floor. There was a bathroom right next to the stairs, just to his right. He closed the door behind him.

He saw another door on the other side of the kitchen. He walked over to it and peered through the doorway. It led into a small living room, where Aoife, Gerry, and the two captives were. The captives were sitting on the sofa, still bound, with the pillowcases over their heads. Aoife and Gerry stood in the room with their guns in hand.

He turned and went back into the kitchen and set the rifle down on the table, then pulled out a chair. He sat down across from Dermot and set his hands down on the smooth surface. He followed the swirling grain with his eyes and then his finger. It was an absent-minded movement. He stopped as soon as he realized what he was doing.

Dermot was thinking about something else. "What are we doing?" he asked, looking at Ray. There was loss in his voice—despair. Ray looked back and didn't respond. He wondered if Gerry and Aoife had heard the comment. He hoped that they hadn't.

Ray knew that Dermot was weak and could be played if need be. But he too wondered what they were doing. He wondered what the exit strategy was. They were now sitting cooped up in a cottage in the countryside with two captives held at gunpoint. They had nowhere to go and no one to turn to. Things were quickly falling apart.

He could see just one outcome for the captives, and he figured that Dermot was thinking the same thing. He looked again at the gun on the table between them. Dermot was looking at it too. He was not a killer, Ray thought. He was not a man who was born for this life. It was a life that he'd inherited, that he'd been dragged into—that had been forced upon him. This was a life that Ray had chosen, and he was beginning to wonder why he had.

Liam was a man of principle and that was why he fought. Gerry was a killer by nature. He had that in him. If he had not been born here, he would have killed for something else, Ray thought. Slowey was much the same way. It was not the glory or the money that Slowey sought but the power and the pain. He was a man of cruelty. Ray wondered about Aoife.

She came through the doorway then. When she stepped into the room, Aoife set her gun down in the corner against the wall. She looked at the two men sitting at the table for a moment before pulling out a chair to join them. When she did, she sat down and shook her head. She didn't have to speak because they all knew what she was thinking.

"It's bad," Ray said. Aoife and Dermot didn't speak. They sat and listened to Gerry pacing back and forth in the next room over, his heavy boots causing the old wooden floorboards to creak. Ray could picture him carrying the gun and watching the frightened huddled figures on the couch.

"What do we do now?" Dermot asked.

"We have to talk to John."

"Ring him," Dermot said. "There's a phone on the wall."

"What's Thomas's phone number?"

"I'll just do it," Dermot said.

Ray watched as Dermot crossed the room and dialed the number. He thought about the situation. They had a man and a woman tied up in the sitting room with pillowcases pulled down over their heads. Soon, they would shoot them and bring the bodies somewhere to dispose of. No one had said it yet, but he knew that it was the only logical action to take. Ray knew that he could save them if he wanted to—that he could stop it all.

Dermot spoke into the phone briefly. He spoke to Elizabeth first and then to John. It seemed that every time he tried to explain the situation, he was cut off. He eventually hung up, having said nothing of value. He turned to them and shook his head. "He didn't want to hear anything," he said. "He mustn't trust the line."

Aoife stood up. "Let's go back in there," she said. "He's alone."

Ray stood up too and they all moved from the kitchen into the living room. Gerry was standing in front of the captives.

He turned when they entered the room. "Did you ring John?" he asked.

"Yeah."

"And?"

"He didn't want to hear anything about it. Not on the phone."

"So?"

"So, we're on our own."

"Let's take them outside," Ray said. He was conscious that the prisoners could hear everything they said. He also knew that they couldn't shoot them in the cottage unless they planned to burn it down and, given the material, that didn't seem like an easy task.

Gerry looked at him. "Right now?"

"Let's get this over with. We need to find out what they know."

Gerry grabbed Joe beneath the arm and pulled him up, raising him to his feet. "Get up."

Aoife moved closer and pressed the barrel of the gun into the woman's chest. "You too," she said. The woman got uncertainly to her feet. She was unsteady without the use of her arms and with her vision still blocked. They brought them out to the back garden and put them on their knees. The woman choked back sobs.

"What did you tell them, Joe?" Gerry asked.

"Nothing," Joe said. The voice was muffled and broken. "I didn't say anything. It wasn't me."

"Don't play with me."

"I'm not. I really don't know what this is about. Please," he said. "Just let us go."

Gerry stepped forward and pulled the pillowcase off the man's head. There were birds singing somewhere. He stooped low, and touched Joe under the chin, pushing his head up and looking into his eyes. "It'll be a lot easier if you just tell us."

Joe seemed to think about it. "Let her go at least." He was pleading.

"We will," Dermot said. "If you tell us what you told the guards."

"I didn't go to them," Joe said. "They came to me."

Ray exhaled slowly. That was it—the admission that they needed. It meant that he was safe, for now. He wouldn't be questioned himself. Gerry grabbed Joe by the throat. "You worthless s– "

Dermot stepped forward and touched him on the shoulder. "That's enough, Gerry." Gerry released his grip and stood up again. He moved back, stepping away from the captive man.

Dermot turned and said something to Aoife. They talked in hushed tones. Then Joe spoke again. "I know about you, Gerry," he said. His voice was quiet. His eyes flicked to Ray.

Something fell over Gerry's face. "What?"

Joe looked even more scared. "You don't have to do this. I kno–"

Before he could finish his sentence, Gerry stepped forward and kicked him hard in the face. The black sole of the Doc connected with his cheek and there was a crack beneath the slap. The man's head snapped back, and he fell awkwardly, slumping back.

"You fucking rat." Gerry spat on the man's bloody face. He stooped down and thrust the barrel of the gun into Joe's neck with force. "I should put a bullet in you right now."

"Ease up, Gerry," Dermot said, stepping forward again.

"No, fuck it!" Gerry said, standing up again. He was frantic. "What are we playing at? He's just confessed. We all know what needs to happen, let's just fucking end it right now!"

Joe rolled forward and swallowed, choking on blood. "You know what I mean," he said. There was a brief moment of silence and then Gerry lifted the gun by a few feet and pulled the trigger. There were three blasts, fast and sharp. The first round caught Joe in the chest. The second and third were in the neck and head.

Dermot tried to yell something—Gerry or Jesus—but the word was lost in a tangle. He reached forward and grabbed Gerry by the shoulder and pulled him back. The woman began to scream beneath the pillowcase. Gerry turned to her in shock, and it seemed to set in then what had occurred.

"Jesus, Gerry," Dermot said quietly.

Ray looked at Aoife, who was watching with tight white lips and a clenched jaw. He wondered if she'd heard what Joe said. Her eyes were ablaze with anger and fear. "Finish the job, then," she spat.

Gerry looked at her. He opened his mouth to speak but there was nothing there, then he brought the gun up and shot the woman in the head through the pillowcase. It was a single blast and the sound carried for a while in the silence of the woman's scream. Her body fell too and as it did a cloud passed over the sun above and threw the garden into shadows. They all looked up to the sky and watched the cloud pass quickly, and the light returned.

Dermot dropped to a squat, holding the pistol in his right hand between his legs. He brought his left hand up to his face and made a strange noise, then stood again and walked in a small circle. "Now what!?" he shouted.

"You knew what you were signing up for," Gerry said.

Dermot turned hard. "I came into this to make Ireland better!" he shouted. "Not to tie a woman up and shoot her in the fuckin' head!"

"What else was I supposed to do?"

"We don't even know what he told them now!" He squatted again, choking. "Ah, Jesus! I don't even know her name!"

Aoife was quiet now, looking at Gerry with sadness. Gerry looked to Ray for support, but Ray was looking at the two bodies on the ground. Gerry followed his eyes to the bodies, and then the rest followed. They stared at the bodies too and then Dermot dropped his pistol to the ground.

"Jesus Christ," he said.

"Alright," Ray said. "We have to finish this. We don't know that no one heard those gunshots. We need to move these bodies and go."

Chapter 26

He could go to the embassy, he thought. It was the only thing that really made any sense to do. If he made his way to Dublin and walked into the American embassy, they could verify his identity and pull him out of the country. To do so would be to throw away the entire operation, though, and the Company might begin to consider him a loose end.

Aoife was lying on the bed beside him with the white sheets half-covering her porcelain skin. Her body was soft and rounded. It was not the best he'd had but it was good, and he felt guilty when he compared it to others so he knew that he cared about her beyond it. He looked away to the window. He knew that he cared for other reasons, too, but he was bitter and defensive and up against the ropes.

Ray had fallen for his mark. It was a cliché. It was a death sentence. He wanted to take her to the coast somewhere and live together in peace, with the sound of waves crashing on rocks below to drown out the creeping anxieties and fears. He wanted nothing more than to run away from it all and to take her with him, but he knew that it was not possible.

The end of the operation was the end of the line and it seemed to be growing closer all the time. Things were spiraling out of control. He wondered if he'd tell this part in the debrief.

He might leave out the woman. Then again, if it made the news, he might not be able to. With the leaks and the media and the mess that was public opinion today, it was harder than it once was. It was television that did it—government and war became a spectacle like never before. They put together investigations and hearings like football games.

He was being bitter again because he was scared, and that was the truth of it. Things were quickly getting out of hand, and he didn't know what direction to go. His goal had been to put guns in the hands of Irishmen so that the Libyans or the Soviets couldn't. That was all. So far, he had been successful. They were in control of a major influx. Guns were flowing to the North. That was all that mattered.

Aoife exhaled and shifted position. She turned and the sheet moved and exposed her thigh. Ray reached over and put his hand on her abdomen. Her skin was soft and warm. He left his hand there for a while, feeling the heat. Then he rolled over and moved down to lay his head on her. He felt the heat of her skin against his cheek and closed his eyes.

Her breathing was regular and steady and he tried to match it with his own. It was soothing, healing. He felt the threat of tears welling inside. He exhaled, breathing slowly. All he had to do was make the right decisions when the time came. He had to think with his head and not his heart—he needed to survive, first and foremost.

She was a tool—a means to an end. He could never forget that. They all were. The entire country was, for that matter. He suddenly felt that Aoife was awake. He lifted his head and turned it. She was looking down at him. Her eyes were open. "Are you ok?" she asked.

"Yes." He thought about Gerry, about the words that Joe might've been about to speak. He knew that, whatever they were, Gerry had had no choice but to pull the trigger. He thought about the last time he had killed too. "What happened between Gerry and Michael?" he asked.

She looked at him again. "What?"

"You know, before all of this."

"Why?"

He shrugged. "I don't know."

"Nothing," she said. She paused. "Michael didn't treat me right and Gerry scared him. That's all." She stared absently for a while. He knew that she was thinking about her cousin, about the execution. "We should get up," she said, eventually.

"I guess we should."

They were at Thomas and Elizabeth O'Shea's. They were staying there because they did not know if it was safe to go home. They'd slept through the day because they hadn't the night before. Then they slept restlessly through the night too. Ray sat up and turned away from her. He threw his feet off the bed and stood, then quickly dressed, pulling on his jeans and sweater.

He picked up the rifle leaning against the wall beside the door and then turned to look at Aoife, who was still in bed. She was sitting up against the headboard now with the sheets over her, watching him. Thomas and Elizabeth had gone to Roscommon to visit Elizabeth's sister. It hadn't been a scheduled visit. "You probably don't need the gun," she said.

He looked down at it and smiled. "Force of habit, I guess."

She didn't smile back. He could see that her mind was at work and that the things that were bothering her would not easily be quelled. "Go on," she said. "I'll be down in a bit."

Ray began to set the gun down against the wall but then thought twice about it. He took it with him when he left the room. He shut the door behind him and walked down the hall to the stairs. There were pictures on the wall, old and new. He went down the stairs and stepped into the kitchen.

Gerry was sitting at the table drinking coffee and reading an old newspaper. He looked up and nodded. "Morning."

"Morning, Gerry."

"There's coffee on the counter."

"Thanks," Ray said. He set the gun down against the wall in the kitchen and then walked over to the counter. He found a mug in the cupboard and made himself a cup.

"I'm starting to get the feeling that there's something going on between you and my cousin," Gerry said.

Ray looked up, then saw Gerry's face and laughed. "Fuck off," he said. Gerry shook his head and looked back down at the paper. Ray finished making the coffee and sat down at the table. "Where are the others?" he asked.

"They're fixing the gutter at the back of the house," Gerry said. "Thomas is too old to get up on that ladder now."

"What do you think's happened to Tommy?"

"Slowey?" Gerry asked. He took a drink of coffee. "He'll be alright. That guy's like a cockroach. He'll outlast us all."

The door opened and Dermot and John came back inside. At the same time, Aoife started to come down the stairs. They met in the kitchen. "Good morning," Dermot said.

"Get it sorted?" Gerry asked.

"Yeah, there was nothing to it."

"What were you at?" Aoife asked.

"Fixing the gutter."

"You didn't want to help, Gerry?"

"I thought I'd leave it to the young."

Aoife filled the kettle and put it on again. "What's the plan, John?" she asked.

"I'm waiting to hear from command," he said. "We'll just have to hold out here for now."

"Are you making a pot?" Dermot asked.

"I can, if you'd like."

"That'd be lovely."

Aoife took the teapot and rinsed it with warm water and then set it down on the counter. She put two bags into it and waited for the kettle to boil. John and Dermot put their jackets over the backs of their chairs and sat down. John picked up the discarded sports section of the paper that Gerry was reading.

Dermot lit a cigarette. "Will you put on the radio there, will you?"

"Was there a please in there somewhere?" Aoife asked.

"Please."

Aoife reached over and turned on the radio. It was a talk show, and it didn't seem good but she adjusted the volume and let it play. The water soon began to boil, and she filled the teapot, then set it down on the table. "You'll have a cup, John?"

"I will."

She set down three cups and then sat down at the table beside Ray. Through the window, the blue sky was clear. The phone rang. They all looked up together. On the third ring, John put down the paper and stood up and crossed the room to it. He picked it up.

"Hello?" He paused and listened for a while. "Alright, Thomas. Thanks. Love to Elizabeth. Yeah, take care now. Bye. Bye now." He hung up the phone and turned to the table. The expression on his face was hard to read. "We were in the papers," he said. "Gerry and Dermot and myself."

There was a silent response.

"It's about Joe and your one," he added. He walked to the table and sat back down.

Ray put his elbows on the table and leaned on it. There was fear around the table. "John. You've been through this all before," he said. "How does it look to you?"

John reached out and lifted the teapot and began to pour three cups. "There was a day you could shoot a man on the street of Dublin city and ride away on a bicycle and disappear," he said. "It's a harder thing to do now. I've been through worse, but it is a tough auld spot we're in."

"How do we find our way out?" Dermot asked.

"For now, we wait."

"We can't stay here. We're not ten miles from *Misneach*," Gerry said.

"What'll they do? Search every farmhouse in the county?" John shook his head and set the teapot down. "We wait until we hear from the command. That's the way war's always been done. Right, Raymond?"

"I suppose it is." Ray lifted the coffee cup and took another drink. It was weak. He set it down.

"Were you ever in a spot like this over there?" Dermot asked, looking at Ray.

"Where? America or Vietnam?"

"In Vietnam, I meant."

Ray shook his head. "It was different there. We were out there alone in the dark, surrounded by the enemy. Mosquitos the size of a *sliotar* and chinks crawling out of tunnels in the muck."

"Don't call them that," Aoife said.

Ray looked at her. "Old habit."

"You go in there with your guns and bombs what do you think they're going to do?" She was aggravated.

"That's what I'm saying," Ray said. "It was different there. That's why we lost that war. This is your war. This, here. This is your strength."

"You're one of us now too," Aoife said. "Don't forget it."

"What are you saying?" Dermot asked.

"We're sitting here in a farmhouse in the country, invisible," Ray said. "If they come down on this one, we move to another one, and then another one. And then when they turn their back, you strike again. And then you disappear. That's your war," he said. "The war of the flea."

"That's how they fought you there?"

"That's how they fought us there. And how they fought in Cuba and in China. That's the new way of war everywhere."

"That's how we've always fought," John said. "There's nothing new about it. That's the flying columns." He gestured at Ray. "Have you read that book there?"

"Which book now?"

"The one by Tom Barry," John said. "There's a copy in there somewhere. I've seen it before."

Ray shook his head. "I haven't."

"You should read it," he said. "You'd get something from it with all that. He was the commander of a flying column in Cork."

"I'll read it."

"You'll like it," John said. "It's a good story too. He was out in Babylon or somewhere like that shooting Arabs for the British Army and read about the Rising in the paper. Like a lot in those days, and these days too, he didn't know much about the history of Ireland, about patriots and imperialism. Well, when he saw that he started learning and when he came back after the war he joined the IRA."

"Be warned," Aoife said. "John'll just keep on with this if you let him."

"You'd do well to listen a little more," John said. "That's your history."

Dermot lifted the teapot. "Heat up, anyone?"

"I'll have a drop," John said. Dermot poured into his cup.

"Aoife?" he asked.

"Sure. Thanks a million."

Dermot topped up his own as well and then set the pot down. "We could be a lot worse," he said. It was as if he was convincing himself of the fact.

"We could," John said. "Ah, we'll get through this alright. *Tiocfaidh ár lá.*"

"What does that mean?" Ray asked.

"Our day will come," John said. "Hugo told me they've started to say it in the Maze."

Chapter 27

"The order just came down to set off a bomb in Blacklion," John said.

"Are you joking?" Aoife asked.

"They want to send a message for his assassination."

"Why Blacklion?"

"It's on the border. There's a checkpoint there. They want to make a statement."

It was early morning, and they were all sitting in the front room, except for John who was standing at the door. He stepped in and sat down in the empty chair closest to the television. He sank into it like a tired man, and it seemed that the air escaped him when he did.

They had been doing little but watching television and drinking and playing cards. There was a football in the lawn and they'd kicked it around the night before. Ray found a copy of *The Odessa File* in the bedroom and was making his way through the first pages slowly.

"I thought you didn't trust these phone lines," Gerry said.

"I don't."

"So, how do you know the army won't be waiting for us in Blacklion?"

"I don't," John said. "But that's the order."

There was silence. It sat in the room for a long time. They looked at one another and listened to the low sound of the television droning. "What's the plan then?" Gerry asked, leaning forward in his own seat.

"There's a man will meet you in Cavan with the car. All you've to do is leave the car where it needs to be and see that it goes off."

"Why can't the man just do it?"

John's face darkened. "Because that's not the orders we were given."

"When does it need to happen?"

"Tomorrow."

"That soon?"

"Aye, that soon," John said. He paused. "It won't take all of you. Just two. Gerry and Dermot, the two of you will do it."

Aoife shook her head. "No," she said. "Ray and I should do it. Seeing as they don't know us yet."

"No, it should be us," Dermot said. "It's my brother locked up and it won't do any harm to us now. If it's a checkpoint they'll have a camera, and your faces will be on the telly before the day's out."

"We should all four go," Ray said. "Two in the car being left and two in the other with the guns. That way we can keep an eye on things. They'll be looking for blood themselves now."

"You're right," John said. "It's best to stick together. Power in numbers."

"You'll stay here, though," Aoife said.

"Too right I will."

Ray leaned on the arm of the sofa. This was not a Company operation as it usually unfolded. Normally, there were hierarchies of command with closely monitored communication channels. Allies were well-placed. Any men he could turn to here however, were so well hidden that he'd never find them. The Company had grown paranoid. Operational security resembled a labyrinth. He was part of a great plot—a master plan, or so he had been told—yet, his perspective was limited, incomplete.

The Sligo Brigade had the same nature. It was a cell—isolated. John was the tower, picking up signals from the Southern Command. Other than that, they operated alone. That, too, was paranoia. There were leaks, moles, and informants throughout the body of the organization. He had been told that they went all the way to the top. It was easy to believe.

He and the Sligo Brigade were guinea pigs both. The command was experimenting, and they bore the brunt of the confusion. He looked out the window past the television. He could see the slope of the grass. He saw the road below and the field on the other side. He looked at Aoife beside him. She was staring absently.

The image of the woman lying in the garden came back to him. It was the pillowcase. He saw that baggy white form and the white stain. He thought, too, of the boy in Laos. The dull slap. Joe didn't bother him in the same way. That was the nature of war. "Anyone for coffee?" he asked. "Tea?"

"I'll have tea," Aoife said.

"Tea," Ray said. "Anyone else?"

"Yeah," John said. "Thanks, Ray."

He got up and went into the kitchen. He turned on the radio and then lifted the kettle. "Streets of London" was playing on the radio. It was tinny and distant. He turned on the tap and filled the kettle. He leaned on the counter and listened to the song and the dull drone of voices in the other room.

When he went back into the other room with the teapot, John had a map out on the coffee table and was marking out a route with a pen. "You'll pick up the car here," he said. He circled a point on the map. "I have the directions written down." He ran the pen along a road and then circled another point on the map. "And here's Blacklion. That's the best route to take."

Ray set the teapot down and went back into the kitchen for cups. He took four from the drying rack and brought them into the sitting room and put them down beside the pot. "There."

"Thanks," John said. "I was just showing them the route you'll take. Dermot will drive there and then Gerry will take the new car from Cavan to Blacklion. I want you to take the lead on this, Gerry. You've done it before."

Gerry nodded. It seemed that no one else but Ray had heard what Joe said to Gerry before his execution. If doubts existed in their minds, nobody dared to voice them.

"Have you been to Blacklion?" John asked. "Gerry and Ray have, I know."

"I have," Dermot said.

"Just past Fagan's newsagent is at the far end of Blacklion. That's where the car's to be parked. You'll see it."

"Not at the checkpoint itself?"

"That's the place. You abandon a car at the checkpoint, you'll be shot."

"A warning will be phoned in?" Aoife asked.

"Of course," John said. "But that's where command wants the bomb to go off."

They planned out the operation in detail. It was a welcome distraction from the murder that had been committed days before. Ray enjoyed this part of the work. It was like a puzzle—a game. They detailed entry and exit points and the routes to and from the site in case of emergency.

Dermot's van would be parked in a nearby industrial lot. The unit would arrive in Blacklion in two separate cars, one of which contained the bomb. Two of them would be in each vehicle. That was for security and because it seemed less suspicious. Blacklion would be under careful watch, but they couldn't keep their eye on every car.

Dermot and Gerry would leave their car parked outside Fagan's and then meet Aoife and Ray at the intersection on the corner, where they would be watching from their own vehicle. Aoife would drive and Ray would stay ready in the backseat with his rifle, because Aoife knew the Irish roads and Ray was more experienced with the gun.

After the bomb was left, they would drive to the industrial lot and change vehicles. The car they took would be burnt out in the lot. They would drive from there directly back to the O'Shea house, where John would be waiting. They would then move on together, leaving after dark to take refuge in another house in another county.

The rest of the day was slow. They watched traffic on the road. They ate together and watched television and the awareness of what waited for them at the end of the night sat heavily on them all. There was a persistent fear that things would come crashing down before nightfall. Yet, it remained quiet. When Ray and Aoife went to bed, the sky had still not darkened.

Chapter 28

Dermot drove them to Cavan. It took nearly two hours on small roads that weaved between small lakes and tight fields. Trees dotted the landscape in clusters between the hills and fields. There were fences, hedges, long grass, and wildflowers.

The roads were narrow and carried them through tunnels of shrubs and hedges which seemed to bury the car. When the wall of green broke, there were hills and houses. Though the country was small, it was no mystery to Raymond anymore how a man could disappear forever in it.

They did not speak much as they drove. Raymond sat beside Dermot and Aoife and Gerry were in the back. The radio played but the signal was often poor. It came and went. They reached Cavan and drove to the address that John had given them. It was a flat near a nameless village along the road.

The flat was on top of an old grocer, which was no longer open. The windows were foggy and covered in dust. Dermot pulled into the back, where there was a small parking lot between the grocer and a football field. There were two other vehicles in the parking lot—a small maroon car and a white delivery van. Dermot stopped beside the van.

Gerry got out of the car and walked to the stairs which he took up to the second floor. He knocked on the door. When the door opened, a middle-aged man opened it. He was balding and had a round white belly emerging from beneath a GAA jersey that once must have fit him. He shook hands with Gerry and then scratched his crotch through his jeans and stepped outside.

They descended the stairs and the man looked at Dermot's van but said nothing. He brought Gerry over to the maroon car and unlocked the door. He spoke with Gerry for a while beside it and then handed him the keys. They shook hands again and the man turned away and walked back up to the flat slowly. He made it up the stairs with great effort and went back inside.

Gerry opened the back door of the car and took a shoebox out. He carried it across the parking lot to the van. As he neared, Dermot and Aoife got out of the van. Ray opened his door and stepped out too. He shut the door and met the group at the front of the van. "That's the car?" Dermot asked.

"It is." Gerry set the box down on the hood of the van and glanced up toward the road. He took the lid off the box. There were two handguns inside. Gerry took one of the guns and slipped it into his coat pocket. He handed the other one to Aoife and then put the lid back on the shoebox.

"All set then?" Dermot asked.

"Yeah." Gerry had two sets of keys in his hand. He looked at them, then handed one set to Dermot and one to Aoife. "Those are for the other car," he said.

Dermot handed the keys of his van to Gerry in return. "I'll drive alone," he said.

"No," Gerry said. "That wasn't the plan."

"I know," Dermot said. "But when I was sitting here watching your man I started thinking about the reliability of the equipment. That could go off on the way up and we'd minimize our losses if I was driving alone."

They all looked at him for a while after he spoke. The sound of distant traffic carried from a road somewhere out of sight. Eventually, Aoife spoke: "If we don't trust the equipment, nobody is getting in that car."

"We stick to the plan," Gerry said. "Two in each vehicle." He handed the keys of Dermot's van to Aoife. "It'll be fine." He put his hand on Dermot's arm. "They don't take chances with these anymore."

Dermot's face looked a little pale, but he said nothing else. He walked with Gerry to the car on the other side of the lot and they both climbed inside. Aoife went around the hood and opened the driver's door. She climbed into the van. Ray got in the passenger side.

Dermot pulled the maroon car out onto the road and Aoife followed close behind. Ray tried to gauge how much distance they would need if the car did explode and wished that he was driving rather than Aoife. He knew that he could not tell her to give more space, though it was only logical to do so.

It took them close to another hour to reach the industrial lot that John told them about. Dermot looped back twice searching for it on the back roads. They pulled in. By then, it was growing dark. There was a chain-link fence around the lot. It had an empty warehouse and abandoned equipment and debris. A white Ford was sitting in the middle of the lot.

Aoife pulled in. Dermot idled on the road. She shut off the engine beside the car and opened the door. Ray got out too. Aoife unlocked the door of the Ford and got inside. Ray climbed into the passenger seat. She started the car. The engine rumbled to life with ease. Then she pulled past the van and back out onto the road behind Dermot, who began to drive again.

Ray watched the rear-view mirror, wondering if they were being watched from somewhere. The plan had been given to them last minute, but it was clearly well orchestrated. The timing was likely to avoid leaks, he thought. They were no longer trusted. They drove for another fifteen minutes and then Dermot began to slow.

They drove into the town. It did not take long to see the checkpoint—soldiers, Land Rovers, and barbed wire. From the main road into town, down the stretch of small buildings lining the road on either side, Ray could see four soldiers. He knew that there would be far more.

"Shit."

Aoife turned her head quickly. "What?"

"I forgot the rifle in the van."

Her lips parted. Her jaw hung loose. "Are you joking?" she asked.

"No," Ray said. "I didn't take it when we changed cars."

"Eejit," Aoife said.

"Give me the pistol," Ray said. "The one Gerry gave you. It's got longer range than mine."

Aoife reached down into her coat pocket with her right hand, keeping the left on the wheel. She handed the pistol to him over the console. It was a Colt 1911. "That'll do you a world of good," she said. "How could you forget the rifle?"

"It was in the backseat …"

"You'd better hope we don't need it."

Dermot turned the corner and pulled onto the road where the newsstand was. Aoife pulled onto the road behind him. Ray took the silver revolver out of his coat pocket and handed it to Aoife. She took it from him and slipped it into her own pocket.

The maroon car was making its way up the road. They could see the newsagent ahead. It had a green facade and white writing across the front. There were other cars parked along the road and a few people walking on the street. "What about the warning?" Aoife asked, looking at Ray.

"Pull over at this corner," he said. "You don't want to get too close."

Aoife slowed the car. As she did, Dermot's car jolted suddenly. She slowed further. "What's going on?" she asked.

The car jolted again and then stopped at the edge of the street about four doors down from the destination. "It looks like he stalled it," Ray said.

"How could he do that?"

"That's what it looks like, right?"

Aoife pulled over to the opposite side of the road. "What should we do?"

The car ahead stayed immobile. They could see Dermot and Gerry moving frantically inside. Then the side door opened and Gerry got out. "What the hell is going on?" Ray said.

"I think we should go check." Aoife started to shift.

"No. Leave the car here," Ray said. "We shouldn't bring it any closer." She opened her mouth to respond but then simply nodded and left the car parked. "Wait here," Ray said.

"No. I'm coming."

"Don't be stupid."

Aoife opened the door and got out of the car. Ray swore. He opened his and stepped out too. Gerry was walking across the street towards them, his face panicked and white. "It broke down," he shouted across the street. "It just won't start."

A couple further down the road turned to look at them. Ray shook his head and waved Gerry over. "Come here," he said, trying not to sound angry. Aoife walked further up the street, moving closer to Gerry and the car. "Aoife," Ray said. "Stay here."

She looked over her shoulder at him. Gerry jogged halfway across the street. "What do we do?" he asked. The three of them were soon standing together in a cluster in the middle of the road.

"Just tell him to leave it," Ray said to Gerry. "Aoife, get back in the car. Leave it and let's go." Down the street, he could see a parked army vehicle. "Let's go. Now."

Dermot opened the door and got out of the car. He shut the door behind him and started to walk away from it, moving toward them. There was a strange expression on his face.

"Aoife, start the car. Let's go!" Ray said. He pushed her toward the vehicle. She glared at him but began to walk. "Let's go, Gerry." He grabbed him by the arm and pulled him closer to the curb. They moved to the footpath. Aoife was just ahead, walking toward the car. Dermot made it halfway across the street.

Chapter 29

The explosion was early. A small blast rocked the car first. The windshield went when the surge of curling flame burst through; buckling doors next, and then the expansive thrust blew the car apart.

The window shattered on the gift shop behind the car and the wall crumbled beneath the impact of the blast. Pieces of metal flew wide, cutting deeply into whatever they connected with. Ray felt small shards scrape against his cheek as he stood across the road and looked on.

Dermot turned sharply. The force of the explosion caused him to stumble, and he tripped over his own feet landing hard on the road. His shoulder hit first and his arm twisted beneath him. He scrambled to his feet quickly, glancing over with wide eyes.

Before he was on his feet, two soldiers rounded the corner of the butcher shop at the end of the block. They were running. Their eyes went to Dermot immediately. One shouted. The other already had his rifle raised. He took a knee and opened fire down the street. The crack of the gunshots seemed quiet in the wake of the explosion.

Ray knew that the soldiers shouldn't have been on this side of the border, but he also knew that he should never have been in Laos—and never officially was. He knew that these things mattered little if the story was managed right in the aftermath. His ears were ringing.

Dermot ran hard. The gun rattled and bullets peppered the road around him. The second soldier lifted his rifle and joined in, pumping rounds at the fleeing man. Aoife cried out and drew the silver revolver from her coat pocket. She ran toward them.

"Wait!" Ray yelled. He reached up to grab her arm as she passed but she already had it pointed at the soldiers. She pulled the trigger. The gun kicked in her hand and the round flew wide, striking the wall of the shop behind them.

The sound of the returned shot caused the soldier's gunfire to pause as the barrels were realigned. The two men looked young, crouched in the street in their khakis with their rifles shouldered. Their eyes were wide with panic and reflected the small flames of the car.

The guns began to rock in their hands again. Bullets began to pepper the walls near the volunteers. Someone was screaming further down the street and the shrill wail filled the air between the bursts of gunfire.

Ray grabbed Aoife by the arm and pulled her hard, dragging her to cover behind a parked car. Gerry ran beside them and dove for cover. Ray pushed Aoife. She stumbled and hit the side of the car, falling behind it. Bullets punched through the windows.

As he fell behind the car, Ray saw Dermot jolt in the street. He drew a deep breath. Aoife was sitting up against the car with the revolver in her hand. Her face was white and there were tears in her eyes. Gerry was desperately trying to pull his Browning from his belt.

Ray reached under his coat and pulled his own pistol from his waistline. He felt the gun in his hand and exhaled slowly.

The rattle of shots subsided. He wondered if the soldiers were out of ammunition or simply waiting for a target to appear.

"We're pinned down," he said. "We need to move."

"Not without Dermot," Aoife said.

Ray scooted over and lowered his body to the ground, looking beneath the car. In the distance, he could see the bent legs and black boots of the soldiers. He shifted slightly, looking past the tire, and saw Dermot lying in the middle of the road.

Dermot was pale and his body was limp on the ground. Ray sat back up and looked over at Aoife. "He's been hit," he said.

"What?"

"He was shot."

Aoife tried to stand. Ray grabbed her arm. Gerry was leaning over, looking at him now. His own eyes were wide and he had the pistol in his right hand. "Is he …?"

Aoife struggled to free herself of Ray's grasp. He held her arm tightly, holding her down. "Stop!" he said. "We need to be smart. They're waiting to shoot."

On cue, a short burst rattled from one of the guns. The rounds pumped into the car. The metallic thuds were loud behind them. A bullet came through the side of the car and ricocheted off the wall across from them.

"Gerry and I will open fire. Run," he said. "Get the car started."

Aoife shook her head. "We aren't leaving him there."

"If he's alive, we won't. But we need the car started." He looked at Gerry. "Ready?"

Gerry nodded slowly. He seemed stunned and immediately began to stand. Ray twisted around the front of the car and pulled the trigger on the Colt twice, firing at the soldiers to distract them from Gerry's sudden appearance. The rifles opened up again.

Aoife broke away from the side of the car and ran for the Cortina. It was not far. Ray pumped two more rounds from the gun, then turned away from the soldiers and returned to cover. Gerry was shooting over the roof of the car at the soldiers in the street.

Ray reached over and tugged hard on Gerry's pantleg. Gerry ducked down beside him. "They killed him," he said. He knew that he had to be blunt or they wouldn't get out alive. They'd die fighting for a dead man.

"He's not dead," Gerry said.

"He is," Ray said. "He's not breathing."

Gerry's face was in agony. "How the fuck can you know that?"

Shots erupted again, slapping into the metal shield. Some punctured it, passing close to the men. "We have to move!" Ray shouted. He pushed Gerry's shoulder. "Go! Go!"

The Irishman looked at him for a moment longer, then scrambled to his feet and ran. As he did, Ray rose and took aim over the roof again. He shot twice more in the direction of the soldiers, not taking the time to aim, then turned and ran after Gerry.

His heart beat and his feet pounded pavement. He heard the explosion of gunfire again and the sound of the impact with the stucco wall he was passing. Aoife was already on the way to them in the Cortina. The falling sun shook across the hood. The vehicle skidded to a stop in front of Gerry, tires squealing.

Gerry grabbed the door handle closest to him desperately and pulled the door open, then threw himself inside. Ray reached the car and pulled open the passenger side door. He climbed in and pulled it closed hard.

"Dermot?" Aoife asked. Her eyes were wide and panicked.

"He's gone," Ray said. "Go!"

"Wh–"

"Go!" Ray shouted, slapping the dash. Aoife hit the gas and peeled around in the road, turning the car back to the direction it had come from. Tears were running over her cheekbones as she straightened the wheel and hit the gas harder, letting the engine roar. The car took off, heading out of Blacklion.

A final burst of fire came from the corner of the street. A round smashed into the side mirror on the passenger side, causing the glass and plastic to shatter, debris expelled away from the side of the car. An army Land Rover tore through the intersection ahead, passing perpendicular to them. Ray knew that it was only a matter of time before it turned back.

Aoife tore through the intersection, moving past the few road signs that marked it. The Ford rattled onto the narrow road on the other side and continued to move fast. She guided it along the winding road and turned off when she could. Ray had his eyes on the rear-view mirrors constantly. Gerry was silent in the back.

They reached the industrial yard and Aoife stopped the Ford beside the van. They climbed out of the car and went over to the van. Gerry opened the back doors and took out a gas canister. Aoife grabbed the other and they doused the Ford in gasoline. They dropped the empty canisters on the ground beside it.

Gerry got into the van and moved it to the road. Aoife uncoiled the long, soaked sheet and lit it. Then they ran to the van and climbed in. Gerry pulled out onto the road and began to drive away from the industrial yard. Ray listened carefully, waiting for the sound of an explosion behind them.

"Dermot's dead?" Aoife's voice was quiet in the backseat.

"Yes," Ray said.

"How do you know?"

"I saw him die," Ray said.

"He was shot?"

"Yes."

"You saw it?"

"Yeah, Aoife. I did."

"And you, Gerry?"

Gerry shook his head. "No. I didn't see it."

"Did you see him after?"

Gerry shook his head again. Ray could feel Aoife's attention turn to him again over the back of the seat. "I saw it, Aoife. He went down. He wasn't breathing."

"He might have been hurt."

"He was dead."

"How the fuck can you be so sure?" Aoife asked. Her voice was sharp.

"I saw it," he snapped. "I know what it looks like when a man is shot and killed. I've seen it too many times."

There was a brief and strangled sob. "Oh my God," Aoife said. "What are we doing, Gerry?"

It was dark and the shadows of the buildings and branches around them fell repeatedly across the front of the van. They continued to drive and eventually Ray realized that he had not heard the explosion and did not know if the car had been destroyed. It was behind them now, he thought. There was no going back.

Chapter 30

The van was moving quickly, scraping branches hanging low over stone walls, swaying with the tilt of the road, corners tight, suspension rising and falling, carrying over bumps and alterations. The evening was dark. Reflections of the inside of the car played on the glass over the dull shadows of the outer world.

Behind him, in the driver's seat, was Gerry. He was staring through the windshield without expression, hands clenched on the wheel. Even in the dim reflection, Ray could see the white of his knuckles. "Slow down."

Gerry looked in the rear-view and then over at Ray. "It's alright," he said.

"Slow down," Ray repeated.

The van rounded a bend in the road and a wooden hut with corrugated metal siding came into view a short distance up the road. A stack of sandbags sat in front of it and the silhouette of a soldier standing behind it could be clearly seen. He was peering toward the approaching headlights with his hands on his rifle, ready and afraid.

"Shit," Gerry said. "Ah, fuck." He slowed the van.

"Turn around," Ray said.

"They'll chase us."

"Turn around," Ray said. "They'll kill us or worse. There's no way we get through that checkpoint."

Aoife leaned over the seat with the pistol in her hand. "Keep going," she said. Her voice was calm and cold.

"What?" Ray said, twisting in his seat to look back at her.

"How many are there? Three at most. We need to run it."

"There's no way we make it."

"If we turn now, they'll know we're running anyway. They'll cut us off or chase us down. At least this way we'll have the edge."

The van was steadily moving closer to the checkpoint. Ray knew that she was right. The soldier held up his hand as the vehicle neared. The headlights bathed the metal and sandbags and revealed a second soldier standing beside the checkpoint.

Gerry slowed to a stop in the middle of the road. One of the soldiers moved up to the side of the van that Ray was on and began peering through the windows. The other soldier moved up alongside the driver's window.

Aoife lowered her arm and hid the gun beneath her leg. The soldier was staring at her through the glass, then paced around to the back of the van to look through the back window. Gerry lowered his window and the soldier looked him up and down.

He looked past Gerry to Ray and then back at Aoife. The soldier who was behind her moved around to the other side of the van and paced up along the side, still peering through the windows. "Papers," the soldier said, turning his eyes back to Gerry.

As soon as his eyes shifted, Aoife raised her arm and brought the pistol up over the seat. She aimed it at the soldier's face and pulled the trigger. The shot filled the car and Gerry flinched hard. The soldier's head snapped back and he dropped out of view.

Aoife turned sharply and pointed the pistol through the window at the second soldier, who stared in shock. She fired twice through the glass, which shattered. Gerry hit the gas and began peeling through the checkpoint. Dust and gravel lifted from the road and sprayed the metal walls of the shack.

"Fuck!" Gerry said. He slapped the wheel with both hands. "FUCK!"

"Just drive!" Aoife yelled.

Ray lowered his window and tried to look for any movement at the checkpoint that was quickly disappearing in the side mirror. "Turn off the road as soon as you can," he said.

The vibrations of the wheels on the road seemed heightened. The van moved faster, veering around tight corners. Grass and shrubs along the edge of the narrow road whisked along the side of the vehicle.

Ray held the Colt pistol in his hand, palm wrapped around the handle. His finger sat in the small curve of the trigger. He watched the rear-view and his eyes moved between Aoife and the black empty road behind them.

To the right, just ahead, a small lane broke off from the main road. Gerry took his foot off the gas and turned sharply, cutting across the small strip of grass. The van jolted hard and dipped, then lifted and tore up onto the smaller lane.

"Where does this road go?" Ray asked.

Gerry shook his head. Aoife leaned over the seat, still holding her pistol in hand. "Just keep driving," she said. "Take the next lane. Keep heading north."

"Yeah, until this runs out and we're left sitting at a dead end on the sea."

"Well, what else can we do?" Aoife asked.

"You shouldn't have shot those soldiers," Gerry spat.

"What was I supposed to do?"

Gerry slowed the van as an intersection became visible in the low light. The road ended and met another running perpendicular to it. A small stone house sat empty on the other side of the intersection. The grass was growing up along the bottom and the windows were broken.

A pair of headlights appeared on the road somewhere far behind them. The yellow light shook through the night. Gerry guided the van to the left and continued to drive. His eyes were on the rear-view mirror. "Do you see that?" he asked. Aoife and Ray did not reply. It was already clear.

The road carried them through houses and hedges into a web of walls and lanes. The headlights turned at the intersection and swept up toward them. "Is it a Land Rover?" Gerry asked. Aoife turned and looked out the back at the lights. "Can you see?" he asked. His voice was weak.

"No," she said. "It might be," she added. "It looks boxy. It could be a van."

"What do I do?"

"Keep driving," Aoife said.

"Oh, Jesus Christ, they killed Liam and Dermot and now we're all going to die," Gerry cried, eyes locked on the reflection in the mirror. His hands were twisting around the steering wheel helplessly, wringing.

"Pull yourself together," Ray said, looking across at Gerry. He was surprised at the man's weakness and panic, his inability to handle the pressure.

"Easy for you to say … you were in goddamn Vietnam."

"Tommy told me you were hard men. A different breed."

"Fuck off."

Aoife leaned over the seat and put her left hand on Gerry's shoulder. "He's right, Gerry. You need to calm down. Just keep driving. We're going to be alright."

"Pass me that rifle," Ray said, looking over his shoulder at Aoife. "Under the seat." Aoife drew back and disappeared from view. He slipped the pistol into his coat pocket. She reappeared, passing the gun awkwardly over the seat to him.

They continued to drive along the road in silence as the light came through the trees. It was dim blue and the moon was shimmering. The leaves rustled and the van rose and fell with the contours of the earth, shaped and molded by man.

Light pierced the back window, casting a white glow through the vehicle. It bathed them all. Ray knew that the people in the vehicle behind could likely see just their silhouettes, yet he felt entirely naked and exposed. The white light shook with dips in the road—the thrust of suspension.

The vehicle behind them was faster. The light continued to grow stronger through the rear window. Gerry and Ray did not look back. Behind them, Aoife could not resist. She turned and stared into the headlights, trying to make out whatever lay beyond them.

"It's … them."

"You see them?" Ray asked, turning then.

Aoife shook her head. "It's fucking them, Ray. You know it is."

Ray stared past her, through the rectangular window at the back of the van. He saw the light. He saw little else. It darkened all around it—submerged all else in shadow. He clutched the AR tightly, feeling the stock and the handle and the long barrel of the gun. He had his finger on the trigger, waiting.

It was time to cut and get out, Ray thought. To take Aoife and go—south or wherever. He could leave it all behind and they could live. Always on the run. Butch Cassidy and the Sundance Kid. Bonnie and Clyde. The vehicle behind them was growing steadily nearer and the beams of the lights grew steadily stronger. It was clear that it would catch or overtake them soon.

"Pull over," Ray said, looking at Gerry.

Gerry turned his head. "Are you mad?"

"They'll catch us if we don't," Ray said. "If we pull over, and the vehicle passes, we have nothing to worry about."

"They'll kill us on sight," Gerry said.

"They'll catch us either way," Ray said. "If we keep running, it'll be on their terms. If they're soldiers, I'll open fire."

"What do you think you're going to do? Blow holes in that tank with your little fucking machine gun?"

"That's been your whole war, hasn't it?"

Gerry continued to look back and forth between the man in the seat beside him and the road ahead. He knew that Ray was right—that they had little choice but to pull over. The vehicle was bearing down. "Aoife?"

She leaned across the seat again. "Yeah, pull over," she said. "I don't know what else we can do." Her eyes turned back to the vehicle behind them. She had the pistol in her hand, finger on the trigger.

Gerry immediately eased off the gas and tilted the wheel slightly, rolling toward the side of the road. The van jolted over the uneven shoulder. There was little room. The vehicle behind slowed with them. There was a moment where the lights just grew stronger. Then heavy machine gun fire erupted.

Glass was punctured and shattered. Holes beat through the thin metal walls of the van. Gerry screamed out in pain and kicked down hard on the gas. He'd already shifted, though, and the van just screamed with him.

"Get out!" Ray yelled. He wrenched his door open and fell out of the van, landing hard on the grass. He rolled down into the deep wet ditch beside the road. The cold puddle seeped through his clothes. Aoife's door opened and she scrambled out of the van too.

The vehicle stopped alongside the van and the gunshots continued. Round after round punched through the windows and walls. Ray held the rifle tight and looked up at the van. Aoife was moving along the side of it with her pistol in hand. "Aoife!" he screamed.

She did not look down. He saw the bullets punch through the vehicle and pass over him. Some hit the hedges and some ricocheted off stone. Gerry did not get out of the van. Ray knew that his body was mangled and tattered in the front seat, slumped against the console or steering wheel, whatever secrets he harbored dead with him.

"Aoife!" he shouted. She was pressed against the back wheel well. She looked down to him, her eyes panicked and wide. The rounds suddenly stopped. Ray rose slightly and began to crawl along the ditch. He made his way closer. He waved his hand, gesturing for her to move. "Come on," he hissed.

Four soldiers came around the van, two on each side. They had their guns out and immediately trained them on Aoife. "Gun down!" a soldier yelled. Ray touched the trigger and had the impulse to fire—he had to restrain himself. There was no way he would kill them all. If he shot, Aoife would die.

Without hesitation, Aoife dropped the gun. Ray watched from below. They swept in and threw her against the side of the van. She cried out in pain. But they did not shoot. He didn't know why they let her live—maybe they saw that she was a woman, maybe they had orders from above.

One of the soldiers gave the ditch and grass a quick sweep with a flashlight but the light did not fall on Ray. Then they moved as a unit, taking Aoife with them around the van. Ray could see the bullet holes and shattered glass. Through the still open door, he saw Gerry's body slumped in the seat, hand desperately extending, grasping for something lost forever.

Ray began to crawl away from the van and the soldiers behind it. He made his way up the wet grass to a broken and disintegrating stone wall and a cluster of overgrown shrubs. He rested about twenty feet from the road. He could see the van and the Land Rover behind it, and the soldiers around it.

Aoife was in the back of the vehicle. The four soldiers were talking beside it. One of them began to speak into a radio. The dim sound of their voices carried. After a moment, two of the soldiers broke away from the group and stepped up to the van, shining their flashlights through the window.

One of the men opened the door. They searched the vehicle quickly with their lights, then stepped around the van and began to shine their flashlights into the ditch again. They swept them back and forth, this time more carefully. A soldier called down from the Rover to them. One answered. The words were lost.

They knew that someone was unaccounted for, Ray realized. They were looking for him. They would not want to risk leaving someone behind. He knew that they probably also wanted to get out of the Republic as quickly as they could. He wondered which would be the stronger driving force. They moved down into the ditch, lights still aglow.

The sky was growing lighter. The two soldiers on the road got into the back of the vehicle, likely speaking to Aoife. He leaned against the wall with a throbbing ankle and the AR still firmly grasped in his right hand. She was right there, he thought. He could save her. It was still possible. If he did, there would be no going back. He would not be able to go back to the Company. He'd be on the run, forever.

If the soldiers moved any further, he would need to move too. They were moving beyond the ditch and their lights were sweeping the hedges and fields. He eased himself along the wall, moving carefully. He could see the men now—see them as men. He saw their young, hardened faces and their paratrooper uniforms.

Ray stood and quickly climbed over the short stone wall, holding the rifle in his hands. He stepped down on the other side and took cover. The slight shuffle of feet carried to him. In

222

the distance, he heard the rippling engine of a motorcycle on a distant road. He heard lorries then, too.

He raised himself and peered over the wall. The men were at the top of the ditch. The bullet-ridden van was on the other side. Behind that was the Land Rover. He set the gun on the wall and knelt. His finger caressed the curve of the trigger. It was gentle and slight. He saw the torso of the closest man down the sights.

Ray drew a breath, took aim, and tightened his finger on the trigger. The man had just started to turn back to the road as the shots hit him. The short burst of rounds caught him in the shoulder and neck and sent him spinning to the ground. He fell into the ditch and disappeared from view. The sound of the rifle hung in the air.

As the second soldier brought his gun to his shoulder and twisted in shock, Ray fired a second burst. This time, the first few bullets missed the mark. He adjusted mid-fire and pumped the rest of the burst into the soldier's stomach. He squeezed again and put another three rounds into the man as he fell.

The soldiers on the road were out of the Land Rover. He saw the two men looking around in a panic and opened fire over the van. It was a mistake. The men were too far and his aim was off. He heard the ding of metal as the bullets hit the van and the Land Rover and buried themselves in the road.

The soldiers returned fire. The rattle of gunfire filled the night. He dropped low and waited for the shots to stop. When they did, he rose again. In less than a second, he had the barrel of his rifle resting on the wall, stock against the curve of his shoulder. He made eye contact with one of the men. The man was looking up at him past the barrel of his own gun.

The barrel flashed. Shots pumped into the wall beneath him, sending a shower of chipped stone into the air. Ray squeezed the trigger too. A burst erupted. The man below ducked behind the van. As he did, Ray brought the gun up and peered down the sights. As soon as he found the second soldier, he squeezed again.

The rounds caught the man and he jolted back, collapsing on the road, hidden from view. Ray lowered the rifle and scanned the road. He could smell the gunpowder in the air. The sound of shots lingered. A bitter aftertaste. He heard a vehicle. Headlights bathed the road to the left.

A second Land Rover rounded a bend half a kilometer up the road. It was coming their way. Then he saw Aoife. She was running across the dirt road, nearly to the ditch on the other side. Her hair was cast back in the breeze and she looked free. The soldier emerged from his position of cover behind the van and began to chase her. He had the rifle in his hands.

Ray took aim. He drew a deep breath, let half of it out, and fired again. The first shot missed but the soldier slowed and turned. He froze, standing in the road. The headlights threw light on him and the van. Ray pulled the trigger and let loose another burst. The rounds caught the soldier high in the chest and sent him back, landing in the dust.

Aoife reached the ditch and ran down into it. She stumbled in the grass and fell to her knees but then scrambled to her feet and managed to keep moving. She made it through the ditch and to the field. The Land Rover skidded to a stop in the road and the doors flew open. Three more men poured out of the vehicle.

Gunshots erupted from the nearest two. Bullets peppered the wall, tearing fragments from it, ricocheting across the field. Ray dropped down beneath the wall again, rifle cradled to his chest. In his mind, he saw Aoife running across the field, making her way to safety—to freedom. He shuffled down the wall. There was a pause in the gunfire and he rose again, spinning to take aim.

He heard the shots immediately. He felt a searing burn in his left shoulder and he fired again. The rounds scattered the two men who remained beside the Land Rover. The third was stooped over the dead man in the middle of the road. He continued to fire, squeezing the trigger continuously, spraying bullets into the side of the vehicle. As long as he was firing on them, they were not chasing Aoife.

The three men repositioned themselves. One lay prone on the road and began to fire on the wall. It was dark and he knew that they could not see him well. It did not seem that they paid any notice to Aoife's escape. The three men continued to fire on his position. He felt a sharp impact and dropped down behind the wall again.

He slumped low, staying in cover. His upper back was pressed against the wall and his legs were splayed out in front of him. He was bleeding heavily. He could feel it. He didn't know where he'd been hit but felt the strength draining from him. His arms felt heavy and weak. He heard another burst of gunfire from the road and listened to it.

He let out a long, deep breath. He could still hear the distant traffic—vehicles on a road not far from here. He wondered if Aoife had made it away. He hoped that she kept running, that she didn't turn back. He hoped she'd know enough to leave him behind. He scooted down the wall a little further and rolled over, lying on his stomach.

Ray crawled to a break in the crumbling old stone and, still keeping low to the ground, peered down to the road. He was not much further. He saw the flashlights sweeping the wall. He saw two of the three men in position, ready to fire. It would take mere seconds for them to notice him, he thought.

He lined the closest man up in the sights and pulled the trigger. The gun went off in his hands again. The men shifted position and opened fire. This time, he didn't move. He continued to pump rounds until the gun ran empty in his hands.

By the time it did, one of the men was on the ground. But, he felt that he had been hit again. This time, more than once.

Ray rolled back behind the wall and propped himself up against it with the empty rifle lying across his lap. He hoped that he had given Aoife enough time to get away. She had a long way to go. There was a derelict cottage, black and dark, some fifteen feet ahead. He pushed himself off the wall and began to crawl towards it. He was weak and tired.

It seemed to take him a long time to reach the cottage. His body was dragging over the rough ground. There was grass and stone and muck. He carried the gun with him even though it was empty because it felt foolish to leave it behind. When he reached the building, he crawled through the doorway. Like a grunt in Vietnam.

It was a small room. The stone walls were nearly collapsing around him. The wooden slats and stairs were broken and rotten. The floor was gone, if it had ever been there, and the grass was growing up around him. He sat up and leaned against the wall, his back to the road and the soldiers on it. He sat back with the gun still in his hand and waited for the men to find him.

He sat for a long time, staring at the emptiness ahead. At a certain point, he thought he heard the engine below. He thought he heard voices too. But the men did not come and eventually he stopped wondering if they would at all. If they came, they would come. If not, he would lie there still. He thought then about his Buick Riviera and back roads. Some faceless girl in jean shorts, tan legs wet from the river, glistening in the moonlight coming through the open window.

He did not know how long he lay there for. It was cool and quiet. He thought about Laos too, a place he never should have been. He thought about the women there and thought that was the worst of it. Then he remembered the dead boy and the amber light, the dull slap, the gun in his hand.

After some time, a cat crept into the abandoned cottage. It appeared on the other side, looking at him with curiosity, cautiously. It was white and small and seemed comfortable in the wild. It moved slowly. The gunshots had frightened it. But it was brave—it had re-emerged. It moved toward him, placing its tiny paws with care.

Ray leaned his head back against the wall and watched the animal. He felt his right hand release the gun, which drooped to the grass beside him without noise. The grass was thick and soft even inside the house. He waited, looking at the cat without moving. The animal watched him from a distance for a while and then began to move nearer.

The countryside was quiet and calm. The air was still and cool. The sky held the evening blue and the moon was giving light to the earth. The light was caught by the cat and its fur was aglow. The cat stood beside him and then cautiously approached his feet. It smelled and nuzzled his sole.

The animal rubbed its shoulder against his boot, then ran the length of its torso along, feeling the touch. It turned and nuzzled in, then rubbed up against his boot and ankle again. He felt a slight twinge of pain but ignored it—he did not want to scare it away.

The cat turned and twisted at his feet, nuzzling and rubbing. He allowed it to. He gave it control. It worked its way past his feet and up his ankles, keeping contact with his leg. It passed his knees and came up along his waist. It stopped and looked at him, waiting. Its eyes were wide and full of care. It nuzzled against him again, and then sat down.

Ray petted the cat and it gave him comfort. He watched the narrow almond eyes nearly blink and the ears twitch. He watched the slight curve of the mouth—a smile. For a moment, as he sat hunkered down against the wall, he felt as if he might cry. He could not understand why but he did not question it. It was the cat and him and a relationship ever so brief and ever so real.

The cat sank in and faded into sleep, entirely trusting. It knew nothing about him. It knew nothing of Laos or Aoife or Ireland. He let his fingers run through the soft fur and felt the response from the animal. He felt good knowing that he was the cause of pleasure. He felt the rumble of the purr, the immediate and uncalculated response from the animal. It was natural.

The smart thing to do would have been to leave it all behind, he thought. He should have left the gun in the grass and found his way to the nearest town. He could have taken a bus to Dublin and found the embassy. He could have left the country. But instead he had thought about Aoife.

Soldiers would return to the site of the gunfight. He knew that much. Police would come—intelligence services. He needed to move on. He took his hands away from the cat, which stirred and looked up at him with sorrow. His right hand found the AR and he closed his fist around it. He willed his legs to stand but they would not move and so he simply lay there, resting back against the wall of the abandoned cottage with an empty rifle in his hand. His head fell back against the stone, and he could see the stars in the denim sky through the gaps in the roof above. He let go of the gun and his hand found the soft white fur again. He could feel the animal's warmth in his palm. There was a gentle purr as it nestled in. It fell into his body, letting its weight rest on his thigh and hip. There was a connection between them, authentic and whole. The fur and belly were soft. The purr was deep. The cat needed him and he it. He felt love. He felt it in his chest and his gut and then there was nothing and he was gone.

About the Author

Luke Francis Beirne was born in Ireland and grew up in Western Canada. His first novel *Foxhunt* (2022) was compared to an early le Carré thriller. Ghostwriter of more than a dozen genre novels, he has contributed to many publications such as *Honest Ulsterman*, *Hamilton Arts & Letters*, and *Strange Horizons*, including the award-winning story "Models." Luke holds a Master's in Cultural Studies & Critical Theory from McMaster University. He lives in Saint John, New Brunswick. *Blacklion* is his second novel.

Also from Baraka Books

FICTION

Foxhunt
Luke Francis Beirne

Almost Visible
Michelle Sinclair

Maker
Jim Upton

Blinded by the Brass Ring
Patricia Scarlett

Shaf and the Remington
Rana Bose

Exile Blues
Douglas Gary Freeman

Things Worth Burying
Matt Mayr

The Daughters' Story
Murielle Cyr

The Nickel Range Trilogy
by Mick Lowe
The Raids
The Insatiable Maw
Wintersong

NONFICTION

*The Legacy of Louis Riel,
Leader of the Métis People*
John Andrew Morrow

Keep My Memory Safe
Stephanie Chitpin

*After All Was Lost, The Resilience
of a Rwandan Family Orphaned
on 6/04/94*
Alice Nsabimana

Montreal and the Bomb
Gilles Sabourin

The Great Absquatulator
Frank Mackey

*Cities Matter, A Montrealer's
Ode to Jane Jacobs, Economist*
Charles-Albert Ramsay

*Mussolini Also Did A Lot of Good,
The Spread of Historical Amnesia*
Francesco Filippi

Waswanipi
Jean-Yves Soucy

*The Einstein File, The FBI's Secret
War on the World's Most
Famous Scientist*
Fred Jerome

*Montreal, City of Secrets,
Confederate Operations in
Montreal During the American
Civil War*
Barry Sheehy

Printed by Imprimerie Gauvin
Gatineau, Québec